The Society
In
Opposition
To
Everything

Santosh Kalwar

UNELMA PUBLISHERS

Published by:

Unelma Publishers
Nuijavuori 1 D 29
02630 Espoo, Finland
email: unelmapublishers@gmail.com

UNELMA PUBLISHERS

The Society In Opposition To Everything

ISBN 978-952-65257-3-0 (softcover)
ISBN 978-952-65257-4-7 (hardcover)
ISBN 978-952-65257-5-4 (PDF)
ISBN 978-952-65257-6-1 (EPUB)

BY THE SAME AUTHOR

NOVEL
That's My Love Story

SHORT STORY
Where the Pandemic Started

NONFICTION
Nature God
Human Behavior on the Internet
Conceptualizing and Measuring Human
Anxiety on the Internet
Quote Me Everyday
Gags and Extracts
Nothing Shakes the Smiling
Heart
Why Nepal Fails

POETRY
A Very First Book of Poems: Heartbreak...
109 Quotes, 07 Poems and a Song of
despair...
20 Love Poems and the Economy Crisis
25 Sexy Poems

Yet another Book of Poems

Happening: Poems

I Am Dead Man Alive

You Can

An Aphrodisiac

The Warrior

Obscurity

The Vandana & Other Poems

Warrior of Light

Adventus

One-liners

The Lacetier: a
collection of poems,
quotes, and arts

CHILDREN ILLUSTRATED BOOK

Pinky and Winky

Dedication

This book is dedicated to all young people who love humour, satire, nihilism, and existential topics, and the goal here is to satirize modern society.

Disclaimer

This is a work of fiction. Names, characters, places, events and incidents are either the products of the author's imagination or used in a fictitious manner. Any resemblance to actual persons, living or dead, or actual events is purely coincidental.

Synopsis / Book description

Farley Underwood is a man lost in his own mind, struggling to make sense of the world around him. His thoughts are a chaotic jumble of mismatched ideas and nonsensical notions, leaving him feeling disconnected from those around him. No one seems to understand him, and he cannot quite grasp the workings of the universe.

In his confusion, Farley longs for a simpler world, one where the boundaries between what is and what isn't are clear and unambiguous. He imagines a place where the janitors scour the garbage cans for quarters, and where the rules of reality remain fixed and unchanging. Alas, this is not the world he inhabits. Reality is a fluid and ever-changing thing, shifting and morphing with each passing moment.

Despite this, Farley refuses to give up his quest for understanding. He realizes that his desires may be absurd, but in a world where everything is nonsensical, what is the value of sense anyway? Perhaps the key to understanding lies not in logic or reason, but in embracing the absurdity of it all.

As he wanders through life, Farley remains a perplexed and befuddled figure, searching for meaning in the chaos that surrounds him. He remains open to the possibility of finding something unexpected along the way, whether it be a pile of quarters in the trash or a castle that remains an is instead of an isn't. In a world where absurdity reigns supreme, anything is possible.

Content

Chapter 1

As I climbed the hill, I counted my steps carefully. One, two, three, four... ten. Despite only being ten steps up the mountain, I was already gasping for air like a fish out of water. It felt like the air around me was working against me, stealing precious oxygen with every breath. After pausing to shield my eyes from the intense sun, I looked up at the peak of the hill. I felt disheartened; I wouldn't have been surprised if it had been Mount Everest. However, I had a job to do. I was carrying a stack of fliers under one arm and a clipboard under the other, and I was determined to deliver them all. So, I continued walking, although my feet felt like they were made of lead. Suddenly, disaster struck. The sweat from my forehead dripped into my eyes, causing them to sting like needles. I tried to wipe the sweat away, but ended up dropping all the fliers onto the ground. As if that wasn't enough, a sudden gust of wind blew through and scattered the fliers around me like confetti. I frantically tried to catch them, but they swirled out of my reach. At this point, I must have looked ridiculous: a sweaty, panting mess of a person, flapping around like a bird with a broken wing. However, I didn't care. My mission was important, and I wouldn't let a little sweat, wind, and gravity stop me. It's true that things are always more complicated than you expect them to be.

I saved two or three by stepping on them and pinning them down with my feet. By the time I had recovered from all the salt burning my eyes, most fliers were about half a mile away. So I left them alone, figuring somebody would pick them up and the message would get out that way. I knew this probably wasn't true, but it was nice to think that way sometimes—like when I was a kid. I felt that if I accidentally threw a quarter in the garbage can, the janitor was getting a tip. That kind of thinking is comforting; everything is fair, nothing is for nothing, and it'll all balance out in the end.

I've spent much time thinking of all the quarters I've thrown out. There has been a significant amount, although no more or no less than for anyone else. A pretty average amount, all things considered, but still an awful lot of money.

I started towards the top of the hill again. It really was a terrible hill. By this point, I was half-hoping that I'd get to the top—all sweaty and everything, with the stupid, crappy fliers—and Delaney Fowles would tell me to get out of her house. That was what had happened with all of the *others*, and a small part of me was hoping it would happen this time, as well, just so that I would never have to walk up the goddamn hill again.

But something kept me going; *something,* although I wasn't entirely sure what. I'm always trying to figure out what keeps me going, but I'll finish once I start something. It's undoubtedly not endurance or heroism or anything, but I don't think it's masochism, either. It's not that I *want* to finish; I can't *not*. It's good or bad, but that kept me walking up the hill.

That's another problem with me—I'm never sure about anything. I wish I was, or *say* I am, but I'm not. I have always hoped that some people were convinced about some things—it's another one of those comforting beliefs, the ones that you have when you're a kid. But the truth is that nobody's sure about anything, even though they and I might *wish* that they were.

Even if someone *once* was or is sure about something, their brain is or will be all decayed by this point. Neither the sureness nor the not-sureness *is* or *will* be sure anymore because of what was *is* not and what it *will* not be. It always depresses me to think about how one day my brain will be all decayed, and all the sureness *and* not-sureness will be gone. It pushes the hell out of me every time I think about it.

I was still walking up the hill. I started thinking about the other people I'd visited that day; *adults,* mostly. If they had let me talk to their kids inside, things would have been better for me. I mean, I wasn't trying to recruit the goddamn *parents.*

I really don't like talking to adults. I'm sure this will be problematic later in life—I practically *am* an adult—but adults always give me this *look.* It just about drives me nuts every single time I see it. The kind of look says, "Isn't it time to go *home* now, kid?" All kind and condescending and very polite and very *concerned.* You know. That sort of thing.

And I will admit it. Usually, it *is* time to go home. The problem is, I need to find out when it's time to go home and when it isn't. I've heard some people say I don't *get* things like others. Everyone's always telling me that. That I just don't *get* certain things. I wish I knew what I wasn't getting, but if I *did,* then I would *get* it.

I get things the same way everyone tries or has tried. But I get more stuff than people assume that I get. Most likely, everyone gets more things than people *believe* they get. This is because people's best thoughts get trapped inside their heads. What usually happens is the best views stay holed up in their heads their whole lives, and then when their brains decay, what *is* is a *was,* so it isn't *is* anymore.

People are funny. I don't *get* people like I don't *get* most things. I get myself, but not them. You would've thought that *because* I was a person if I got myself, I would get them. But nobody seems to get each other, and everybody seems to get me even less.

I've always pictured myself sitting inside this castle; it's a *metaphorical* castle, of course, but it's a lot more accurate than any other castle if you think about it. And I open all the doors to my castle and yell at all the people walking by to see if they'd like to come in, but they *don't.* So I don't know if they don't because they don't or don't want to, but they don't either.

I had gotten very deep into thought by this point—about people and how they never know if it *is* or *isn't,* and how they do or don't get things. When I get into thought, I usually don't notice what I'm doing anymore. People do that often—they get deep into thinking—but not as much as I seem to. I've always wondered if maybe I was a bit more like people than people, and that's why I had such a hard time getting the things they got.

When it comes to people, the more you try to make sense of them, the less sense they make. So, the more you get them, the less you get them. So, I got them a little *more* than they called themselves or me, which was why I *didn't* get them. I was hoping that eventually, I would *not* get them enough so that I would get them again because if I figured I could get people, then I could get everything else. If I could figure *that* out, people might stop saying I didn't get things. Then the *is* could become the *is* again, and the janitor could get tips when you throw out a quarter by accident, and everyone would come into my castle.

So that's why I was walking up the hill.

When I got to the top of the mountain, I was so out of my breath that I just sat in the middle of the driveway. If these people had looked out the window just then, they'd probably have wondered what I was doing sitting in their driveway. But I wasn't too concerned about this. Nobody looks out their windows anymore.

I finally got up. I walked down the driveway, which had many potholes for such a lovely house, and knocked on the door. They had planted all these rosebushes out front, but something was wrong with them. They were healthy and green and everything, but they didn't have any *roses.* There was no *reason* for it, but they had decided not to bloom.

I was still looking at the rosebushes when somebody opened the door. I'd never met this girl's mother before, but I could tell she was an amiable person right off the bat. I could tell because she gave me this big smile like she was thrilled to see me, even though I was just some sweaty, emancipated-looking kid she'd never met before clutching a handful of crappy fliers.

"Are you alright?" she asked me. I looked like I was about to pass out.

"Yes," I said. "I'm here to talk to…to…." I reached into my pocket and pulled out my list. "Delaney Fowles."

She looked surprised. "You're here to talk to *her*?"

I hate it when people do that. When you ask them a question, they repeat it like they didn't goddamn hear it the first time, even though you *know* that they did. But I still liked Mrs Fowles less than before. It seems judgmental, but sometimes you can't help things like that.

"I'm trying to recruit her," I told her because I had been silent for a long time, and she was starting to look confused.

"Recruit her?" she frowned. "Oh! Is that what your fliers are for? How creative!"

"Yes," I said, although fliers weren't exactly the most novel idea in the universe. I looked over her shoulder, hoping she'd move to let me in the house. She didn't move.

"What are you recruiting for, Mr…?" she trailed off.

"Underwood. Farley Underwood." I held out my hand. She shook it, even though it was all sweaty. I liked her a bit more again. "I'm recruiting for the SIOTE," I said in each letter. Acronyms are good marketing tools because people usually have terrible attention spans and can't listen to all five words.

"Oh? What does that stand for?" she asked like it was fascinating. She still hadn't called for this Delaney girl and wasn't letting me into the house.

I sighed. "The Society in Opposition to Everything." It was a *joke,* but people had difficulty understanding it so far.

"Oh?" she raised her eyebrows. I'd noticed that she said 'oh' an awful lot.

"Yes."

"What does that do?" she asked. She was getting the "skeptical" voice most adults get when talking to me. I could feel that *look* not too far around the corner, but I wasn't ready to go home yet.

"We go around opposing everything. It's very symbolic." I peered into the house. "Is Delaney not home? I can come back another time."

I don't know if it was because she felt bad for me. After all, she was perplexed, or a bit of both, but she stepped aside and let me into the house.

I became very excited. I didn't usually get this far in my recruitment. When I started down the hallway, I realized I didn't even know where this girl's room *was.* It occurred to me that her mom thought I was her friend, and that was probably why she had let me into the house in the first place. So, then I realized I couldn't go back and *ask* where her room was; that'd give it away. So, I walked down the hall casually, in case her mother was still watching me like I knew exactly where I was going. I got lucky because I eventually came to this door at the end of the hall with a bunch of dents and a ripped-up *Metallica* poster on the front. I tried to push the door open, yet it was locked. So, I knocked very politely.

Someone was in there, but they took their time getting to the door. Then, finally, this girl opened the door after what seemed like an unprecedented amount of time. She didn't look thrilled to see me but didn't seem too bothered.

"Are you Delaney?" I asked her, just to make sure.

She didn't say anything. She looked confused, which was understandable. Finally, she just nodded at me.

"Why did your parents decide to live on a hill?" I asked her. It wasn't what I had planned to ask, but sometimes things like that just float to the top of your mind and pop out. There's really no helping it.

Delaney folded her arms. She was quiet for ten seconds. "Bears," she said eventually.

Now *I* needed clarification. "Bears?"

"Yes, *bears*. My brother was mauled to death by bears when he was a child. That was at our old house. Bears are too lazy to climb the hill, so they leave us alone now."

"Oh," I said, about seventy per cent sure she was pulling my leg. But she had on this sombre expression; I had just met her, so it could've been confirmed for all I knew. So, I said, "That's terrible."

Delaney laughed; it was this very sarcastic, *mean* kind of laugh that she had. But at least it wasn't one of those fake laughs that people give you sometimes. I can't stand those things.

She kept on laughing. I just stood there because I was pretty confused. "It wasn't because of bears," she said finally. "You're sweating. Did you know that?" I was about to answer, but she kept on talking. "What are those fliers? I don't want to join any clubs." She looked rather suspicious. Apparently, she was the kind of person who was very wary of fliers.

"It's not a club," I said, "It's a *society*." I liked society much better because the word *club* carried several bad connotations from childhood that I didn't want to acknowledge. I handed her a flier because I didn't know what else to do.

She read it for a moment. "What does that mean, the 'Society in Opposition to Everything?'"

"It means that we oppose everything," I said. It was really very intuitive.

She stared at me for a moment. Then, "If you oppose *everything*, doesn't that mean you're opposed to clubs?"

"Well, yes," I said.

She paused for a moment. "And *societies?*"

"Of course," I answered.

"Then aren't you opposed to *yourselves?*" She said it in this snotty voice like I hadn't thought of that.

"Obviously," I said.

She frowned. "That doesn't make any sense."

I sighed. This was the reaction I had been getting every time. People didn't understand that it was a *joke.* They got very offended because it didn't *make sense* when there were so many other, more *important* things that didn't make sense that they *weren't* offended by. It didn't make sense to have something that made sense if everything else didn't make sense in the first place.

I *could* have explained this all to Delaney, but she was beginning to look pretty impatient. Things stop being funny if you have to *explain* them to people, especially if they need excellent attention spans.

So, I just said, "We're opposed to things that make sense."

She stared at me for a moment. "You can't be serious," she said irritatedly. She seemed to be slowly coming to a realization.

"We're opposed to things that are serious," I said.

Delaney stared at me for a moment. "How many *members* do you have, anyways?" she asked.

"Oh, I'm the only member," I said. "That's why I'm trying to recruit people."

She looked at the flier, then grinned suddenly. "That's the stupidest goddamn thing I've ever heard," she said. Then she slammed the door in my face.

I knocked again, very polite and all.

"What*?"* she called from inside the room.

"So, are you going to join?"

There was a long silence. Then, when she still hadn't answered, I knocked again.

"Delaney, are—"

"*Of course*, I'm going to join!" she snapped. Then she was quiet.

"Okay," I said, thinking she might pull my leg again. But this was the farthest I'd ever gotten, so I wasn't just about to give up. "I need your phone number, though, so I can contact you."

Delaney didn't say anything. She was annoyed that I was still there because she had finished talking to me. When they're finished talking to you, certain people are *finished*. There's not much to be done about it. I stood there for about a minute and was about to leave when the flier slid back out. It had a phone number scribbled in this terrible, illegible handwriting in the left corner.

"Thank you," I said. Then, I waited for her to say goodbye, but she didn't respond. So, I said, "We'll be in touch with you tomorrow afternoon."

"Stop talking in the *plural*; there's only *one* of you," she snapped. "And get out of my house."

I'm beginning with the part about Delaney because that's where it started and because it didn't really start with *me*. It might have started with all of the stuff I described earlier; for example, the non-senseless and the non-sureness, and the getting going to not-getting and back to getting again, and the *is* and the *isn't,* and whether we do because we do or because we have to or want to do or because we have to don't do or don't want to do. After all, that's how everything starts. At least, probably.

But my thoughts could be more organized. I wish it wasn't that way, but there you go. So even though I *could* talk about the non-senses and the non-getting and the *is* and *isn't* and the yes or not wanting or not having to be or not be doing, I'm not going to talk about those things. So instead, I will tell you what happened so you can better see how I did and didn't figure it out. You may have figured it all out, but if you have, you probably still need to.

So even though *everything* started with those things, that's not where *it* really began; I have thought about this for a very long time, and I realized that it didn't start with those things, it didn't start with me, and it didn't start with Delaney, either.

It started with the hill. And then I had to finish it.

Chapter 2

I only managed to recruit someone other than Delaney, so I went home around six. I could tell that my mother was home from work because she started talking to me when I opened the door.

"Farley, where have you *been*?" she called. I could tell there was company over because she was using that *weird* voice to talk to me. I can't explain it exactly. Her voice would always change depending on whether or not there was company over. I walked to the kitchen only to discover that, sure enough, her whole goddamn *book club* was occupying our sofa.

I turned around to leave quickly, pretending I'd walked into the wrong room. Those people can ensnare you in a conversation for *hours if you aren't careful.* It's really quite remarkable. I am still determining how they do it.

"Farley*,* come *back* here," my mother called. She was using the same voice. "Young man, you need to *communicate* better," she said sternly. "You cannot wander around the neighborhood because I never know where you *are."* She said this diplomatically, like she was the most reasonable person in the universe. The weird thing was she never seemed to care about communicating with me unless there was a group of other people around. So, I always wondered if she wanted me to share with her or just wanted me to *pretend* to communicate with her when her book club was around. I knew I couldn't just *ask* her that; I had tried before, but she had just been offended. I wished she would just come out and *say* it some time, though, because things like that can be confusing.

So, I just nodded in agreement. I tried to leave again, but then the ensnaring started.

"Have you got your *driver's* license yet, Farley?" Mrs Sanchez asked me. Mrs Sanchez had very wispy hair and several grandkids. However, she never spoke about them because it made her feel old.

"Farley's not *old* enough," my mother answered, "He's not *sixteen* yet."

"When's your birthday, Farley?" Ms Wallden asked. Ms Wallden had eight cats and was divorced from her husband. They probably divorced because of the cats.

"His birthday is August the *first*," my mother told Ms Wallden. She always added an extra *the* in there for no particular reason.

"Are you excited?" Mrs Turner asked me. Since the other two ladies had, Mrs Turner probably should ask me something.

"He hasn't prepared for the test," my mother answered. "Farley thinks he knows everything already." She said it jokingly, but I knew she wasn't joking.

I turned around to leave.

"Farley! Don't leave when you're in the middle of a conversation," she scorned me. "That's rude."

I'd never actually *said* anything, but I stayed anyways. Sometimes you can't help things like that.

All of us ate dinner together in the kitchen. Food wasn't allowed anywhere else in the house; my mother was anal-retentive about that sort of thing. She thought that if a crumb fell somewhere outside the kitchen area, the ants, mice, raccoons, and everything would send telekinetic messages to each other and have the entire house devoured by the following day.

I laughed a bit when I thought of that, right in the middle of Ms Wallden's sentence. This earned me somewhat offended looks from all four book club ladies.

"Anything to say, Farley?" my mother asked sharply.

I shook my head.

"Was something that Ms Wallden said *funny,* Farley?" My mother was pretty angry with me, so I assumed Ms Wallden hadn't exactly been making a joke.

"No," I said, "I'm sorry, I just thought of something funny. Something else. That's all. It wasn't what *she* was saying. I'm sorry," I said again, directly to Ms Wallden.

"That's alright, dear," she said in this disapproving voice that told me I *hadn't* been forgiven. Adults always say things as if they are *is* when they are *isn't.* It just about drove me crazy, and to make matters worse, I *still* didn't know what they had been talking about.

"Can I clear your plate, Ms Wallden?" I asked, trying to make amends.

"Oh, that'd be *wonderful*, dear. Thank you." Ms Wallden was the kind of person who always called people "dear," no matter who they were. She thought it made her sound maternal or type or something. I don't know.

I cleared all of their plates and then went to my room. They didn't try to stop me because I thought they were still mad at me. One thing I've discovered is that old ladies are all crazy. If all of us are crazy, then old ladies are the craziest. It's not their *fault.* They can't even help it. It's just how they are.

Chapter 3

I called Delaney after school got out. It rang a bunch of times and then went to voicemail. I didn't leave a message. I never leave voicemail messages because people never call you back.

I waited ten minutes, then called her again. She didn't answer, so I started to walk home. I only live about a half mile away. Once I got home, I saw that my mom was inside, so I hung out on the porch and called Delaney thrice. Finally, she answered.

"Farley, you can't just go ahead and call me as soon as school gets out," she snapped, not even bothering to say hello.

I needed some clarification. "Why not?"

"*Because.* It makes it seem like you're desperate for my membership," she explained. She sounded like she was disappointed with me or something. "You need to make it seem like *I* need the club more than *it* needs *me*."

"It's not a club," I said, "It's a society. And it doesn't really *need* anyone."

There was this long sigh from the other end. "Are you still at school?" she asked eventually.

"Yes," I said. I don't know why I said that. It was just the first thing that came out. Sometimes you can't help things like that.

"Alright. I'll pick you up in ten minutes. Okay?"

"Okay," I said. She hung up, and I walked back to the school, unsure of what to expect. When I arrived, Delaney was already waiting in this big back car at the front of the school. She was reading a book, her feet on the steering wheel, trying to look calm and relaxed. I knocked on her window.

She didn't jump, so she must have already known I was there. She threw the book in the back—very casually, and everything— and then unlocked the car door.

"You can *drive?*" I asked. I was impressed by this.

She didn't answer. "Hurry up," she said impatiently. "I've been waiting here for five minutes. Where were you?"

I didn't want to explain it very much because I figured she'd think I was an idiot. "I don't know," I said. "Groovy car." The seats were all black and made of leather and stuff.

"This is why you can't recruit any members," she explained critically.

I glanced up. "Huh?"

"Because you say things like 'groovy car.'"

"Oh." I paused. "I like saying 'groovy.'" I didn't have any reason *why*. I just did.

"I don't care about *that*. You can use whichever outdated expressions you *want*." She started the car. "You have to act like you're not very interested in the car *or* my driving. You need to act more aloof." She pulled out of the lot. She was a reckless driver because she almost ran over a few freshmen. "You need to act *disinterested*. People *like* you more when you're disinterested. They don't *know* it; it's very subconscious, but they *do*."

"Oh," I said. I was glad that Delaney was helping me with the getting or non-getting thing; she had a lot of advice. I was curious about the car, so I asked, "When did you get your driver's license?"

Delaney sighed, clearly disappointed that I wasn't learning anything. "*Ages* ago," she said. "I mean, I'm *seventeen*."

"You *are?"* I was trying not to act impressed; I really was, but I had never been in a car with a girl before, let alone an *older* girl. This had just occurred to me.

She ran her hand through her hair rapidly, like it was in her way or something. It was weird. "Basically," she said.

"What do you mean, *basically?"* I asked.

"I'm almost seventeen. That's all."

"*Almost?* Like, *when?"*

Delaney frowned. She obviously did not like the way this conversation was going. "Well, in January."

"January!" I laughed. "'It's May, for god's sake. You're not *seventeen.* You're only a couple months older than *I* am."

"Oh, shut up," she said in an irritated voice. People don't like it when you catch them lying about that. They get mad at *you,* even though it wasn't your goddamn fault that they hadn't been telling the truth. "It doesn't matter, anyways. I've got a car and a license—what've you got? A stupid club that nobody wants to join." I was beginning to think she'd only picked me up so that she could insult me.

"It *is* a pretty nice car," I said, running my hand over the leather part.

She sighed. "It's my dad's car," she admitted eventually. "It's not really mine. I don't have a car."

"He doesn't use it?" I asked.

She just shrugged. "No, his company's touring France right now. They sell computer products. Cutting-edge technology and all of that. They're trendy in Europe."

"Oh," I said, but I wasn't interested. "Where are we going?" But, of course, we weren't headed to her house and weren't directed to mine.

"To your club's new meeting place," she responded.

It had never occurred to me that the club should have a meeting place, but it made sense. I sometimes have a problem where I assume that because something is for me, it *is* for everyone else, too. So, I usually forget to make things, so they actually are *is,* which is a pretty big problem." So, you already have a place in mind?" I asked.

She sighed. *"Yes.* We can use it to recruit more members. It makes it seem more official. Have you done *anything* whatsoever concerning the *promotional* aspects of the club?" She sounded very exasperated.

"I made fliers," I said.

"Yes, I s*aw* that. Anything else?"

I shrugged. "I made a list," I said, "Of people who might want to join. But you were the only one who said yes."

She sighed. "How many names were on the list?"

"Twenty-six," I said. I took the list out of my pocket and handed it to her. She started reading it while driving, which made us swerve wildly into the other lane and almost hit a goddamn mailbox. She gave the list back to me and then swerved back into her lane.

"How'd you make this list?" she asked like the whole thing was no big deal.

My heart was still beating quickly from almost being killed, so it took me a moment to answer. "I wrote down everybody whose picture wasn't in the yearbook," I said eventually.

There was a long pause. Delaney looked thoughtful. "Oh," she said.

"I figured that if they weren't in there for sports or music or drama or math or going to dances or anything, they'd have a lot of free time to join my club."

Delaney turned towards me. "Well, don't *tell* me that," she said.

I frowned. "Huh?"

"You can make your lists however you want. But people aren't going to want to join your club if they *know* they're only getting recruited because they weren't in the yearbook." Delaney did that thing with her hair again to get it out of her face; it was like she was mad at it. I would probably get angry a lot if I were her; her hair always seemed to be in her face. Maybe that was why she was such a poor driver.

"They don't want to join *anyways,*" I said, sighing. "I've already asked them." Well, I had mostly asked their *parents.* It had been more difficult than I'd anticipated to gain access to the *people* on my list. Things are always more complicated than you expect them to be.

"That was your biggest mistake," Delaney said, pulling off to the side of the road and putting the car in park before it was stopped. The gears made this grinding noise like they were really upset about that. Delaney ignored it. "You can't *ask* people if they want to join. You make them ask *you.*"

"Oh," I said. This was all becoming much more complicated than I'd anticipated. "So, why did *you* join if I did practically everything wrong?" I was expecting her to say something insulting about my terrible campaigning strategies, lack of a driver's license, or my general lack of aloofness and say that she had only decided to help me because I was pathetic and useless incompetent.

Instead, she said, "Because you walked up my hill."

Chapter 4

After we'd parked, we walked for a while in the woods. I asked Delaney if she thought it was safe to leave her car just parked off to the side of the road like that. She said that it didn't really matter.

After we had been walking for seven or eight minutes I became convinced that we were lost. This was because Delaney wasn't following a trail or anything; she was just kind of walking straight onwards and I was stumbling along behind her. Once I couldn't see the road anymore, I began to get a little bit panicked.

"Are you *sure* you know where we are?" I asked her. "It's okay if you don't, really. I won't think any less of you. You can still be in the club and you'll still have a groovy car and everything, but if we keep walking we'll just get more and more lost then—"

"Shut *up*, Farley, I know where I'm going," Delaney said stubbornly. I began to wonder why I'd agreed to walk in the goddamn woods with her in the first place. She was obviously unhinged. It began to occur to me that she might be a teenaged-female-serial killer, for all I knew, and that if she *was* then she could *easily* get away with my murder; right in the middle of the goddamn forest. My thoughts started whirring around like crazy; I can get very paranoid sometimes. I had begun to toy with the idea of stabbing her with my pen and making a run for it when she stopped suddenly. I almost crashed into her.

"There," she said. "Look."

"Where? I don't see anything." I wasn't looking my hardest, though, because I was keeping an eye out to see if she tried to pull a gun or a butcher's knife or a machete or something. I had really worked myself into a frenzy. My hands were shaking and everything.

"You have terrible eyesight," she said. "Alright. Come on." I kept on following her, figuring that if she *was* going to kill me there probably wasn't a whole lot I could do about it now. All I had was a pen, after all. Eventually, however, I *did* see it; it was this little clearing, with ferns all over the place and these two giant boulders sitting at the edge. The sides that were facing us were all flat-looking, like someone had cut them in half. The clearing probably *would* have been sunny, if it hadn't been blocked by the boulders; but they made it even darker than the rest of the forest.

By this point, I had decided that Delaney probably *had* known where she was going. I let go of my suspicions that she was trying to kill me and stepped out of the woods and into the clearing.

"I don't know about this," I said. "I mean, it's a cool place, but it's a little bit too *quiet* here to actually be oppositional. It's so…*nice* and all."

Delaney smiled; that mean, kind of sarcastic smile that she had; and walked into the clearing as well. "No, you don't get it," she said. "This is very oppositional. You have to be *far away* to be oppositional. Otherwise you're still being corrupted by society. The air is polluted with people's opinions and everything."

I thought about it for a moment, and decided that she really meant that the *isn't* wasn't the *is*. If you are alone, then the *is* is always the *is*. The more people there are, the more you risk the *is* becoming the *isn't;* or, even worse, the *isn't* becoming the *is*. There is always miscommunication and then the *is* is the *isn't*. The less people there are, the safer you are, but you're never completely safe.

That was something else I realized. You're never completely safe because you can't be sure of the safeness, because sureness is never sure, but it doesn't matter because the sureness and the non-sureness are decaying.

For example, if the sureness is that Delaney will not kill me, and Delaney does kill me, it does not matter because she and I have let the thoughts sit in our heads and they will decay all the sureness and non-sureness eventually, anyways.

It doesn't matter if I am dead because if I am dead, I am not, and if I am not then they are not to me, and if they are not to me then she is not to me, and if she is not to me than she did not kill me, and if she did not kill me I am not dead.

If I am dead then Delaney did not kill me because she had to or wanted to, she killed me because she killed me. If she killed me, I am not. If she killed me, she is not. If she and I and the sureness are not, then the janitor is not getting a tip when you throw out the money and it does not matter anyways because the sureness and non-sureness are decaying because we are not.

"*Farley!*"

I felt this jolt of panic when I realized that Delaney was shaking me. Naturally, I assumed that she was trying to kill me, so I panicked and pushed her away. She lost her balance and fell backwards, throwing her hands out behind her to stop her head from smashing against the ground.

I was just staring at her for a few moments. I realized that I must have spaced out, and she was just trying to get my attention. I immediately felt very bad.

"What the hell is *wrong* with you?" Delaney was just staring at me with this look on her face. I couldn't tell what it was. I couldn't tell if she was angry or alarmed or annoyed or amused. It seemed like all of them, and her hands were bleeding.

I blinked. "Sorry," I said. I *was* sorry.

"I was sc*reaming* at you," she said.

"I got into a thought," I told her. "It happens sometimes." It *does* happen sometimes.

She stared at me for about a minute. She didn't get up. Then, this weird smile came onto her face. And she started laughing like crazy.

"You're a freak," Delaney said. She was still laughing. The laughing was very mean, but for some reason it was nicer than most kindness.

"You're mean," I told her. I said this because she was mean.

"You're all fucked up," she said. She finally stopped laughing, then she stood up and stared at her hands. "I hate you. *Fuck* you. You goddamn *idiot,* Farley."

"I know it," I said. "I *am.*"

We just had to start tipping the janitors. If the janitors got tipped when we threw quarters into the trash by mistake, then our brains wouldn't start decaying.

"Do you like this place?" Delaney asked.

It was like I was being snatched back. We had been somewhere and now we weren't there anymore. I had brought us there, and Delaney had taken us back. It wasn't a bad thing, but it just felt like I was less *is* than before.

I started looking at the boulders. I liked the way they put a shadow over the whole clearing. It made it feel kind of protected; like when you hide inside a snow igloo in the winter. It was nice.

"Oh," I said. "I don't know." I was thinking about what she had said earlier; how I needed to act more disinterested. "I mean…there's no *anything* here. Where would we *sit?"*

"Well, we can re*decorate* it," Delaney said. She clearly had this all figured out. "Listen. Where else are we going to have it? In your *basement?*"

I shrugged. "Well, my basement is being refurbished," I said. My mom refurbished our basement every six months or so. "We can hold it in *your* basement, though."

Delaney gave me a very threatening look, and I started to wonder if she was a serial killer again. My mind will often do that; become very convinced of something that doesn't make a lot of sense. She pushed her hair out of her face. "That's what basements are *for,*" she said. "They're *meant* for holding meetings. *Obviously,* we can't meet someplace we're *expected* to. You're not being very *oppositional,* Farley, for someone who founded a club that opposes everything."

"It's not a club, it's a *society,*" I said. I really liked the place. Acting disinterested was harder than I'd thought. "Well, people won't want to *walk* this far," I said eventually, voicing the last of my complaints. "It's too out of the way."

Delaney pushed her hair back again. She did that an awful lot. "Well, to be honest, the reason it's so far a walk is because we walked halfway across town. This is only about five minutes away from my house."

"*What?*" I was severely annoyed now, which didn't happen very often. "So, we walked all that way for *nothing?*"

Delaney sighed. "I couldn't go *home,* Farley. My mother thinks I'm at tennis practice."

I was confused. "You play tennis?"

"No."

I let out a sigh. "Well Jesus *Christ*, Delaney, you could have at least told me. I thought you were trying to *kill* me or something."

She turned around to face me, her arms folded across her chest. "What?"

I turned to look at the boulders. "Okay, you win. Never mind."

Delaney Fowles was an imaginary tennis player. She also might have been a serial killer.

I live inside a castle inside an igloo under the boulders, and I am all fucked up.

Chapter 5

After Delaney and I made it back to the car, she drove me back to my house. I thought my mom would be angry with me; after all, I'd forgotten to communicate with her again; but instead, she seemed very excited.

"Who was *that*, Farley?" she asked. "Was that a *girl*?"

"Yes," I said. She had the goddamn bookclub over again. "Have you finished your book yet?" I asked.

Nobody answered me. "Farley, do you have a girlfriend?" Mrs. Sanchez asked very seriously. These kinds of things are very important to Mrs. Sanchez.

"No," I answered.

"I don't know, Farley," Ms. Wallden said, raising her eyebrows. "That girl was very pretty."

"Okay," I said. I didn't think that Ms. Wallden had actually had a chance to see whether she was pretty or not; Delaney had only been parked in our driveway for about two seconds before she'd backed out way too quickly and almost killed the neighbor's cat.

"Farley, tell us the *truth*," Mrs. Turner said. She felt like she should say something, because the other two ladies had.

So I said, "I don't have a girlfriend."

The three bookclub ladies laughed, while my mom just watched them with this weird expression on her face. I'd seen that look before. It meant that *she* didn't really care whether I had a girlfriend or not, but that she *did* care whether or not the *bookclub* thought I had a girlfriend.

My mother didn't care about the *is* or *isn't*. She didn't care if she could see the castle, as long as everyone else thought she could see it. If her brain decayed it wouldn't matter because it was not *is*; and she was not *is* and she never could be *is* and worst of all, never wanted to be.

"I don't know if I believe him," Mrs. Sanchez said, and the other two burst into giggles.

I was feeling a bit confused. I didn't know why I would lie about not having a girlfriend. The whole conversation had become very uncomfortable and a little bit depressing, and I could feel the ensnaring that was inevitably about to begin. "I have to go to my room," I said, trying to make a quick escape. "I have homework." I heard them burst into laughter again.

"First a *girlfriend*, then *homework*…next thing you know, he'll be running for class president!" I could hear my mother laughing along with them. I closed the door and lay down on the bed, on my stomach. Old ladies are crazy, I swear to God.

I didn't actually do my homework. It's something you have to get into the habit of doing, and I really was *not* in the habit. I guess that I *wished* I was, but I wasn't. Sometimes there's nothing you can do about those kinds of things.

We had this piano keyboard that plugged into the wall. I wasn't very skilled at the piano, but I thought I could be better if we'd had a *real* one. We *used* to have a piano when I was really young; not a great one, but still, a *piano*; but my mom got rid of it because the top was water-stained. Afterwards, I threw a temper tantrum and wouldn't speak to her for three days. I'd always play the theme from Beethoven's ninth symphony on it. Now that I think on it, that might have been another reason she got rid of it.

Anyways, she was angry with me about the temper tantrum; but I think she felt kind of bad, too, because she promised to get me another one for my eighth birthday. I think it must have slipped her mind; she bought me two model airplanes and three different racecars and a toy microscope and new ski boots and two movies and a new bike and a five-layer chocolate cake, but no piano. And you can't really complain about the lack of a piano after getting all of that stuff; *I* certainly couldn't, especially when all of her friends were there and telling me how lucky I was and all of that. You can't really complain about *anything* after getting all of that stuff. Getting two model airplanes and three different racecars and a toy microscope and new ski boots and two movies and a new bike and a five-layer chocolate cake meant that you were very lucky. You see, my mom would always tell me about those kids in South Africa and Somalia and Nigeria and places like that were eating uncooked rice for dinner; so, whenever I thought about *any* of it, it just made me feel like a terrible person.

I had begun to get kind of depressed by this point, so I started playing in a bunch of different minor keys on the keyboard. Minor keys are good because they sound sad and everyone knows it. There's no *why,* they just *do.* They just are *is,* so it's nice.

Then I started to think about all the Nigerian kids dying in the desert because they couldn't cook their rice. It made me feel even worse. I stopped playing the keyboard and figured that I'd probably have deserved it if Delaney *had* been a serial killer after all. That would've been my *fault,* anyways, and it *still* would have been better than dying of uncooked rice.

That was when I realized it; I realized that we were all fucked up because I did not have a piano, and because they did not have rice. If I had owned the castle, I would have cooked rice for everybody and left tips for the janitors. They were not *is* because of rice. I was *is* because I was all fucked up. If they'd had a piano, they would still be not *is*, and if I'd had rice, I would not have eaten it. And would will never even meet each other because I couldn't even figure out how to get people to come into my castle.

That was when the stupidest thing ever happened. I put my face in my hands and started to cry. Not loud crying; just that angry, frustrated crying, that kind when you get that stupid tennis ball thing in your throat and the water kind of forces its way out. That kind of thing happens to me sometimes. It really is inexcusable; you'd think I was a twelve-year-old girl or something.

I swear to god I wasn't crying because I was *sad*, though; it was because I was angry. I was pretty goddamn pissed about those African kids not getting the proper rice that they needed. The problem with me is, when I get *angry*, I start to *cry*, so it's very misleading. You would think I was a crybaby, but I'm really not. I'm just pissed off. I *swear*.

Anyways, my mother chose this moment to barge into my room.

"Farley, that playing was *beautiful*," she gushed. "Will you come down and play something for the girls? I keep telling them that you're very talented." She paused for a moment. "Farley…are you *crying?*"

I shook my head. "Jammed my finger underneath my bed," I said through clenched teeth. I was trying quite hard to stop crying; but it just wasn't working. I had no control over my tear ducts or anything. This just made me madder, so I started crying more. The whole situation was just generally infuriating.

My mother looked horrified. She might not have seen me cry since I was about two. I don't know. "Farley, what's *wrong?*" she whispered. "Did your girlfriend *break up* with you?"

This made me feel a little bit better. I started laughing.

"*Well?*" she asked. She obviously wanted to know.

"Yes, mom," I said. Things were very funny all of the sudden. "My girlfriend broke up with me. "I hate lying; you're making the *isn't* into *is,* and you're doing it on *purpose*; but sometimes you just don't have any choice. I don't even know what would have happened if I'd tried to tell her about the castle thing. She would have institutionalized me or something.

"I'm so sorry," she said, still standing in the door. She stood there for another second, then said, "I'll leave you alone, Farley." Then she closed the door.

My mother would like to watch all of her friends watch her live in the castle. If I bought the castle, my mother would watch her friends watch me feed all of the children rice and tip the janitors.

"He just broke up with his girlfriend, so he's not really in the mood to talk," I heard my mother calling to her bookclub.

"How terrible," Mrs. Sanchez said.

"They poor dear," said Ms. Wallden.

"That must have been difficult," Mrs. Turner said, because the other two had spoken.

I could tell they really wanted me to hear their sympathy and all that, because they were practically *scream*ing their voices were so loud.

"He's up there brooding, but I'm sure he'll be over it soon," my mother said. "You know how boys are."

I was still laughing a little bit to myself because the bookclub was being so goddamn funny. It's a weird thing like that; after you've been crying, the tiniest thing will seem perfectly hilarious. After I was done laughing, I turned over on my stomach and started playing the keyboard again. I had remembered the boulders in the clearing. Sometimes things like that make you feel better, just for no reason at all. You can't even explain it.

There are no doors to the castle, so I broke all the windows. I didn't know what else to do.

Chapter 6

Delaney and I returned to the clearing the next day after school. We didn't have to venture to the middle of nowhere to get there because apparently, tennis only took place there on Tuesdays and Thursdays. Delaney's mother warmly greeted me from outside, waving her arm and calling out, "Hello, Harley!" Despite being far away, I couldn't correct her on my name. Sometimes, there are things beyond our control. Delaney picked up her dad's old lawnmower from the garage and we walked for five minutes through the woods to get to the clearing. She wanted to get rid of the ferns, and although I was initially hesitant, she made a good point about how it would be inconvenient when it rained. After agreeing to her logic, it took us an hour to get the lawnmower started since neither of us had ever mowed a lawn before. Finally, Delaney was able to get it going by inserting a key into a particular spot. But, we were hit with flying rocks, sticks, and pinecones after starting it, and I had to jump out of the way to avoid being hit. When we finished mowing, the lawnmower was in rough shape. Instead of returning it, we left it as a monument on the side of the clearing, assuming Mrs. Fowles wouldn't miss it because they had two other, better lawnmowers. In addition, we discovered that the clearing's floor was made of rock, the same material as the boulders, and that it had been covered with a thin layer of dirt, most of which had been flung by the lawnmower into the woods and my face. This was probably why Delaney's hands had bled when I pushed her onto the ground the day before, which I still felt bad about. However, I knew that saying sorry again would only make Delaney angrier, and I was worried she might be a serial killer because of the rosebushes. So, I chose to keep my mouth shut to avoid any further trouble. It seemed like the safest option.

I suggested to Delaney that we should drive to my house and pick up some of our old dining room chairs, but she rejected the idea and said we should use tree stumps instead. I commented on the potential to look like "lost boys" and she became angry, throwing a pinecone at me and saying that the chairs wouldn't fit the desired aesthetic. We ended up using five tree stumps and a flat rock as a table but struggled with the weight of the rock. Delaney attempted to roll logs to move it, but ended up dropping one on her foot and injuring herself. We went to her house to tend to her wound and her mother jokingly asked if we were too old to be playing in the woods.

Unfortunately, Delaney didn't enjoy being teased in a good-natured way. "We weren't playing mom, it's none of your business!" Her response didn't make her sound more mature, and only served to make her angrier. Mrs. Fowles laughed and said, "Alright, as long as you're having fun," before leaving. Delaney swore again, saying, "God, I hate her!" I peeked into the doorway, wondering if we were talking about the same person. "She's seemed nice enough to me," I said. "Shut up, Farley," Delaney hissed, making a face. "This is why nobody wants to join your club." I didn't think that had anything to do with it, but I didn't argue with her. When someone like Delaney is angry and swearing, and probably has broken toes, you can't argue with them. You just have to let them be. It was then that I realized that Delaney was too messed up to come into my castle, even though she was supposed to be there to take care of the rosebushes. It was ridiculous.

Chapter 7

It started raining the next day, so I suggested that we hold our first meeting in Delaney's living room. To my surprise, Delaney agreed with me. I think her toes were still hurting a lot.

The good thing about the rain was that Delaney didn't have to go to imaginary tennis. Her mom made us lemonade and everything. She said that she thought it was nice to finally meet one of Delaney's friends. She kept on calling me "Harley." I didn't really have the heart to correct her. Sometimes, if someone thinks your name is "Harley" for long enough, there isn't really anything you can do about it.

That got me thinking about college. I didn't have the best grades or anything, but my mom had all this money saved up so I expected I was going to college *somewhere.* I wondered what would happen if one of my professors started calling me "Harley"; just right in the middle of class or something. I wouldn't be able to *correct* him, obviously, because I wouldn't want to interrupt or anything. Then that professor would talk to all the *other* professors about me, and *they'd* all end up thinking my name was Harley. Then once I'd graduated my professors would write me job recommendations and so my *boss* would start calling me Harley, and then all my *coworkers* would think that was my name. And then I'd probably sit next to this really nice lady who worked as a secretary or something, and so we'd get married and name our son Harley, after me. Then I'd probably end up dying of alcoholism or commit suicide because I was depressed about how nobody knew my name. And then on my tombstone my wife and my son Harley would write in big, black letters, HERE LIES HARLEY UNDERWOOD; BELOVED HUSBAND AND FATHER, except they wouldn't actually mean that, because I would have been a terrible father what with the alcoholism and the suicide and everything.

But it wouldn't really matter, anyways, because Harley Underwood would never have actually existed in the first place; so, he couldn't have been a beloved husband and father; and so it wouldn't have even been a lie, after all.

"Farley!"

I was so startled when Delaney yelled at me that I almost fell off the sofa. "Wha...what? What's wrong?" "I've been yelling at you for the past five minutes. You were completely ignoring me. Again." She looked upset about it. "I'm sorry," I said while putting my hand to my head. "I was lost in thought." Sometimes, when I get deep in thought, there's nothing anyone can do to snap me out of it. "Is that going to happen often?" she snapped. I shrugged. "Well, anyway," Delaney huffed. "We need to start recruiting. A club isn't a club unless it has at least three members." Still rubbing my head, I asked, "Why?" "One member is a person, two members is a pair, and three members is a group. In order for there to be a club, there needs to be a group." As I began to wonder if the castle existed if I was the only one in it, I said, "Should we make more flyers?" Delaney glared at me. "No," she said firmly. "Give me your list."

Chapter 8

"So, what are you saying then?" asked Marcia Owens, a very overweight girl who never ate anything and was always chewing bubble-gum. "What are you opposing?" "Everything," I replied. Marcia Owens looked pretty confused and asked, "Well, what do you do? Is it an official club?" "What do you mean, 'official'?" I asked. "I mean, can it go on your college resume?" Marcia Owens was one of those people who didn't want to join anything unless it could go on her college resume. "Of course not," I said. "We're opposed to college resumes." Marcia Owens seemed to think we were pulling a trick on her or something, and she gave us a weird look. "Well, is it allowed?" she asked. "Is what allowed?" I asked. "Are you even allowed to oppose everything?" Marcia Owens blew a really big bubble and then popped it all over her face. "We're allowed to oppose whatever we want," I answered. "It's because we live in a free country—we have freedom of speech." I think Marcia Owens felt patronized because she started to get a bit angry. "No, you can't," she sniffed. "That means you oppose black people, Muslims, and gay people, too. That means it's a hate group. I ought to report you."

"I don't think you understand," I said, pretty sure that Marcia Owens was confused. "The name is ironic." "What?" She still looked pretty mad. "In order to be opposed to everything, we would have to be opposed to ourselves. Therefore, we would have to be opposed to people who are opposed to everything. It's a paradox because it contradicts itself, and therefore it's ironic." "Well," she spat at me. It seemed like she still felt patronized or angry or something. "It'll be pretty ironic when I report you to the principal, won't it?" "No," I said. "I don't think you know what 'ironic' means. Ironic means that—" Marcia Owens spat her gum at me and stomped away. I just stood there, still pretty confused. "Why did we have to ask her?" I demanded, turning towards Delaney. "She wasn't even on my list." "Because you got her to spit her gum at you," Delaney said. She looked pretty amused about the whole thing. This just made me angrier. I was about to make a mean-spirited remark when this stretched-out looking kid with a piercing in his lip, ear, and four other places came walking over to us. He was one of those kids who had really black hair, the fake kind, and was wearing a bunch of morbid-looking jewelry and rings and all that. You know, one of those kids. He looked like someone who could have had a very friendly face if he hadn't obscured it with a bunch of stupid piercings. "What did you do to make her so mad?" the kid crossed his arms. He looked a little bit happy that I'd gotten gum spat out at me. "Is your hair naturally that black, or did you color it that way?" I asked. I asked because I was genuinely curious. The kid looked pretty pissed at me, though.

"She didn't talk to Farley for very long," Delaney corrected, responding to the original question from the kid. "He tends to offend people with what he says." Although I didn't necessarily agree with her statement, Delaney spoke up again before I could defend myself. "So, are you going to answer his question or act like a child about it?" she asked impatiently. The kid looked at both of us and gave a half-smile, which I found endearing. "I dyed my hair black," he admitted, "because I didn't like how it looked when it was blonde. It made me look like a highlighter." Suppressing a laugh, I noticed a group of kids nearby who looked similar to him; although they appeared to be angry, it was hard to tell. "What did you say to her?" the kid asked nonchalantly, rubbing his neck. Delaney responded, "She wanted to join our club, but wc didn't let her." Though I disapproved of lying, I knew better than to mess up Delaney's plan. However, I did interject with one correction.

"It's not a damn club. It's a society," she kept getting it wrong. I was pretty sure she was doing it on purpose. The kid looked unimpressed at this point and asked, "Oh yeah? Which club?" I emphasized, "It's a society. It's called the 'Society in Opposition to Everything'." At that, the kid laughed, and I was glad I got the appropriate reaction. I asked the kid if he wanted to join, liking him because of his laughter and good smile. "We've only got two members. It'd be great if you'd join." Delaney hissed, "Farley, he can't join unless he's on the list," giving me a threatening look. I knew I had done something wrong. The kid muttered, "That's alright," with his friends motioning him to leave. "I've got to get back to-wait, what list?" he asked. "The list Farley made," Delaney sniffed. There was a pause, and the kid asked Delaney, "So, am I on it?" Still looking at his friends, he seemed curious to know whether he was on the list or not. Delaney replied dismissively, "You probably aren't. Maybe. There are only twenty names or so. I don't know. Farley, do you even have the list?" I did have the list, but she already knew that. I started rummaging around in my pockets.

The kid's friends had started to leave. "Listen, guys," he muttered, rubbing his neck anxiously. He didn't want to be left behind and seemed curious about the list. People are always curious about stupid things like that. "Is your posse abandoning you?" Delaney asked him, using an innocent, joking tone with a hint of sarcasm. The kid laughed nervously and rolled his eyes. "I don't have a posse. I want to be considered an individual." He was clearly nervous as he rubbed his neck again. His friends seemed angry and waved him down once more, but he gave them the middle finger and they left. "Those guys aren't really my friends anyway," the kid said, still rubbing his neck. "You have the goddamn list or what? I don't have all day." I had found the list by that point and was holding it out to him, but he kept on talking. "Those guys suck. They're all posers. You got the goddamn list, or what?" "Yes, I've got it," I muttered. "But I need to know your name so I can find you." "If you don't know who the hell I am, why the hell would I be on your list?" He was getting angrier and more anxious. I was about to tell him about the yearbook thing, but then I remembered Delaney's warning. "Look," I said, "You can go after your friends if you want. We don't care."

"Don't tell me what to do," he trailed off, then shook his head. "They're just a bunch of stupid assholes anyway." He gave me a smile that appeared at the oddest times. "What's your name?" he asked, clearly struggling with maintaining his attention. "Oh," he muttered. I raised my eyebrows. "So, uh... do you mind if I look at the list myself?" The boy began rubbing his neck, growing increasingly nervous. "Just to see if it's even on there, you know? This'll be my real name, won't it?" "Well, I'm assuming so," I responded, becoming irked by the pointless conversation. I handed him the list. "Oh," he said, taking the list and holding it up close to his face, like he needed glasses or something. He gave it back to me and announced, "I'm on there," looking quite pleased with himself. "Would you be kind enough to tell us who you are?" Delany asked, growing just as irritated as I was. The boy resumed rubbing his neck. "My last name's Cary," he said, nodding at the list. I glanced down. "Ellery? Ellery Cary?" The boy shrugged and looked at the ground, seeming ashamed of his name. "Listen, Ellery Cary," I said, "do you want to join or not?" I was considering removing him from the list due to his irksome behavior. I was mostly irritated by his lack of care for his name. If he wasn't more careful, he might end up being called something like Emery or Celery and that could lead him to take drastic measures, like committing suicide with the wrong name on his tombstone, for example.

Ellery Cary shrugged and said, "I guess I'll join. Do you mind calling me Seth, though? That's what everyone else calls me." "We absolutely will not call you Seth," I said angrily. I almost felt like punching him. "It's your name, it doesn't matter if you like it or not. It's your name, you moron." I was so frustrated that I almost walked away, but I had to restrain myself since I needed a ride home with Delancy. Ellery looked surprised and said, "Okay. You can call me Ellery, then, if you want to so badly." He gave us a smile that made up for his idiocy to some extent. Delaney warned him, "Once you join, you can't just back out on us. There'll be ramifications. You know. So, I'm not sure if we should really let you in." I was about to ask Delaney what ramifications she was talking about, but she gave me a look, so I stopped myself. "I won't back out," Ellery said sincerely. "Your club sounds great. Your society, I mean. Listen, I've been looking for a way to get away from those guys. They're a bunch of assholes." "It's just that it's a girl's name. That's all," Ellery said, trying to defend himself. "Well, I think we all know you're not a girl," I said. "I'd be more worried about the earrings and jewelry if you're worried about that." Ellery thought

I was joking and gave me a smile, but I was serious. It was frustrating when people didn't take the proper things seriously.

Chapter 9

Delaney and I drove Ellery to the meeting spot where there were boulders. Ellery liked Delaney's car a lot, but he wasn't a big fan of the woods. He explained that he had recently moved there from the city and didn't like getting his Converse shoes dirty. "Wear hiking boots next time," Delaney suggested. I asked Ellery what it was like living in the city because I was curious. "It's the best," Ellery replied. "It always smells good. Like something's baking, you know? We lived right by a bakery in my apartment. My brother lived with me, but he's in college now. He's at Princeton, can you believe that? He's much smarter than I am. I probably couldn't get into Princeton. He got into Stanford too, but he didn't want to go there." We strayed from our original topic, so I asked Ellery if the city was congested. "There's a bit of congestion. There's a lot of cars, but most people in the city don't have cars. It's people visiting and working there that bring in all the cars and everything. We didn't even have a car until my dad got a big promotion and we moved out here. It's terrible. A terrible place, really. My brother Paul was lucky. He went to Princeton before we moved to this terrible place." I wanted to ask Ellery why his parents named one child Paul and the other Ellery, but I didn't want him to feel self-conscious about his name. He also seemed to stray from the topic again, but I suppose some people digress no matter what you do. They can't help it.

"What exactly are we doing anyway?" Ellery asked once we were all sitting on tree stumps. He was looking at Delaney. "Don't ask me," she replied. "Farley founded it." She gave me a sarcastic look as if to say that I didn't have an answer. "We're not doing anything," I said. "We just exist." I realized that the problem with people when they exist is that they start building their own castle. Those who don't exist don't build castles at all. But those who do exist can only build a castle for themselves, which eventually decays and falls apart. "If we can create the 'are,'" I continued, "then we could make a difference and help others. But the 'is' cannot become the 'are' because that's not how we were built. We break things down when we try to force the 'is' to become the 'are.' And if the 'is' becomes the 'isn't,' we cannot become 'are'." Delaney explained to Ellery that I was just lost in thought. Ellery asked if I could hear him, but Delaney suggested that I might be psychotic or something. She then urged him to recruit more members for our cause, even those who he had flipped off before. Ellery looked offended by her suggestion, but I offered to show him the list.

Ellery stared at me for a second and I explained, "I was just having a thought." He muttered, "That's a little rude, you know," as he took the list from me and held it really close to his face. I was pretty sure he needed glasses. After quickly scanning the list he said, "Nope. None of them on here." Although it didn't take him too long to read through it, he could have been lying. Then again, it was probably for the best; the people on the list didn't seem like the friendliest. "Listen, I've got to ask," Ellery said. "How did you make this list, huh? Because it looks like you just put down the names of a bunch of losers." Even though he was giving me that smile again, he looked a little bit put out all the same. "I put down anyone who wasn't in the yearbook," I said, "so that they'd have time to attend all the meetings." I didn't care what Delaney thought. I was through lying. Delaney didn't seem to notice though; she was staring out into the woods, probably still thinking about that boulder we hadn't been able to move. Ellery frowned and said, "Huh. Okay. I guess that makes sense." So Ellery Cary became a part of our club. At this point in my life, I typically brought a peanut butter sandwich, pretzels, and grape juice to school for lunch in a paper bag. I had been putting more peanut butter on my sandwich than usual because my doctor had told me I needed to gain weight. The problem was that if you put too much peanut butter on, it makes your tongue stick to the roof of your mouth, takes forever to chew, and once you try to swallow it feels like you're suffocating or something. One day, I was in the library struggling to eat my peanut butter sandwich when Delaney and Ellery walked up to me. I was curious as to why they were there and a little bit irritated as well. Just because we were in a club together didn't mean they could bother me during my lunch period. Ever since I had realized that what was is couldn't be, I had become disheartened about society in general. I wasn't going to give up, of course, it was like the hill and I had to finish it, but I didn't like other people looking at me while I was eating.

I noticed that Ellery had removed all of his piercings except the one in his ear, but before I could ask him why, I found myself unable to speak. Ellery started talking excitedly about Delaney's idea that we should all eat lunch together in the cafeteria to gain recognition for our club. I felt apprehensive about it all as it was becoming a big deal, but I couldn't express my concerns. Delaney reasoned that it would be temporary and that we could attract new members. I took a bite of my sandwich as Ellery remarked that he had never seen me eat in the lunchroom before. I was finishing my sandwich when Ellery saw that I was afraid of the lunchroom, which led to Delaney's bursts of laughter.

I shrugged once again and raised a finger to explain my behavior. It took me almost two hours to finish eating with them staring at me; the pressure was too much. Eventually, I said, "I don't like people watching me eat. The cafeteria is too noisy, and there are a lot of germs. Plus, I always bring my lunch from home, so I have no reason to go there." They both gazed at me while I opened my grape juice, forgetting it earlier when I was busy eating a peanut butter sandwich. Delaney chimed in, "It will make our club look more official." She stopped laughing and looked annoyed since I wasn't embarrassed, making it no longer a joke for her. I replied, "But our club isn't official, and I don't want it to be official." Delaney gritted her teeth and said, "Yes, but if you want people to join-" I interrupted, "I don't want any official sort of people to join." Delaney sighed heavily and said, "This is precisely why you can't get any members. You're so stubborn, Farley. You're terrible at campaigning." "I don't want to be good at campaigning," I said. "I'm done with all the faking and pretending. It'll only bring us members we don't even want. That's how things go wrong, and it'll be our responsibility." I realized that Delaney needed to stop trying to sell her castle and focus on fixing the rose bushes. "Well, Jesus," Delaney exclaimed. "Don't get all worked up about it."

I tilted my head back in order to finish my grape juice quickly. Once I had swallowed, I slammed the can down on the table. I expected Delaney to be upset but she didn't seem bothered; instead, she appeared lost in thought and eventually walked away. Ellery and I watched her go, and he asked if this meant she agreed with me. I nodded slowly, explaining that if she disagreed, she would have kept arguing. I then took out some pretzels to eat, prompting Ellery to feel uncomfortable and fidgety. I offered him a pretzel, but he declined, insisting that he had already eaten lunch. As I began to munch on the pretzels, he asked if we were even allowed to eat in there, as he thought it was against the rules.

"I said 'no', but I made a deal with the librarian. I had the whole library to myself until a freshman kid decided to copy me. However, I was pretty sure he was afraid of me because he hadn't left the corner since September. He was there now with the top of his head barely visible under a giant book. I could never tell if he was reading it or hiding under it. Ellery raised his eyebrows and asked 'what sort of deal?'. I replied 'If I could eat here, I'd stop stealing the library books.' Ellery stared at me in disbelief and asked if I actually steal library books. I replied, 'No. Otherwise, I'd be breaking the deal.' Ellery continued to ask whether I used to steal library books to which I replied, 'Yes.' Ellery was confused as to why I wouldn't just check them out. I replied, 'Because then I'd have to give them back.' Ellery expressed his disapproval of stealing, but then interrupted our conversation to ask for a pretzel. He then asked if I stole the books to give them a better home. I corrected him and said, 'No. I took them because I wanted to read them.' I found it hard to understand why this was such a difficult concept for him to understand. 'They're books, Ellery, not puppies. They can't have homes.'"

"Oh," he held out his hand absentmindedly again. I put a handful of pretzels in it. The bell rang, signaling the end of lunch period. "Oh crap, I'm going to be late," Ellery just stood there, rubbing his neck. I wanted to ask why he hadn't moved if he was already so late. "Well, see ya after school, Farley, thanks for the pretzels," he gave me a strange wave, then turned and hurried out of the library. I continued to eat my pretzels, still staring after him. He was a strange person, perfectly insane, I swear to God. I glanced back at the kid in the corner. I wondered if he had a castle or if he was inside a castle. I thought about all the people who may be inside a castle but would still never be inside a castle to me, like the children in Africa or the janitors. I pondered on the decay, certainty, and the cycle of starting and stopping again. Not getting. We could not exist. There was nobody else in the castle except me.

Chapter 10

After that, we didn't gain any new members for a while. Delaney didn't complain about it as much as I thought she would. The only thing she seemed mad about was the fact that we still couldn't move the boulder. The three of us attempted, but apparently, Ellery was weaker than me and Delaney. He was always complaining about getting dirt on his shoes, so he wasn't much help. Ellery was amusing to watch but a pretty weird kid. After a few more days, he removed all of his piercings, and he even stopped wearing morbid jewelry. I was concerned because he kept changing what he was. If you change too many times, then what are you? I was worried about the uncertainty and decay. But the worst was probably the decaying before the decaying because that made everything seem less. A significant issue with Ellery was that he always had to go home to do his homework, and he'd finish practically after dark. Finally, Delaney and I informed him that if he wanted to do his homework so badly, he'd have to bring it to the meeting place because he was missing all of the meetings. Approximately a week after Ellery joined, he was sprawled out in the center of the tree stumps on his stomach with four different textbooks open in front of him. Delaney and I were having a conversation while sitting on the stumps. "I'm not arguing with you, Delaney," I said. "I'm just respectfully stating my opinion." "Coyotes are not better than wolves," she responded. "Why not?" "Because coyotes eat dead things," she commented with a disgusted expression. "All that means is that coyotes are more resourceful. Foxes, on the other hand--" "Farley, I think we can all agree that wolves and coyotes are both better than foxes," she interrupted. "Well, they're not as good as coyotes, but I still think they're better than wolves," I countered.

"How could you say that?" Delaney snapped, as if I had terribly offended her. "A fox gave my younger brother rabies." I eyed her suspiciously. "I thought your younger brother was killed by a bear?" "No, that's how he actually died," Delaney responded seriously. "Well, did he die in the woods?" I asked. "Because if he did, a coyote could have eaten him. That would have been the circle of life." Delaney looked at me incredulously. "Why would that be a good thing?" "Because humans always interfere with the circle of life. It's annoying for the rest of the animal population. The circle of life is much more natural," I explained. Delaney rolled her eyes. "No, he didn't die where he was bitten. Rabies doesn't kill you immediately." I decided I wanted to be a coyote - it seemed much less complicated. "Well, I just assumed that the rabies caused him to go crazy and run away into the woods. Otherwise, he wouldn't have died at all because rabies is treatable." "No, Farley," Delaney corrected me. "He died in the garage. He committed suicide." "You just told me he died of rabies!" I exclaimed. "Why did he commit suicide?" "He didn't know that rabies was treatable," Delaney replied. Ellery, who had been studying, interrupted us with a disapproving look. "Do you two have any idea how offensive you're being?" "To whom?" Delaney asked. "To anyone whose brother has died or has rabies or committed suicide or was mauled by bears," Ellery said, rubbing his neck. We all sat in silence for a while, not wanting to offend anyone further.

Ellery suddenly said, "My brother was almost mauled to death by a bear," as if it was an afterthought. "Really?" I asked. Though I was still annoyed with him, that kind of stuff intrigued me. "Oh, yes," Ellery replied, very seriously. "He went hiking with a group of friends from college near some campgrounds. They were either attacked by a bear or saw one. I don't remember, but that's why I don't want to go to Princeton. Too many bears." "You know," I pointed out, "If you went to Princeton, that wouldn't mean you'd have to go camping. In fact, you're probably more likely to get attacked by a bear right now than-" "It doesn't matter," Ellery interrupted, obviously not listening. "I wouldn't get into Princeton anyways. I'm not as smart as my brother." With that, he stared despondently at his textbook and resumed his homework. Ellery was not always the most engaging conversationalist. Things went smoothly for a couple of weeks. I found myself in a pattern - something I'd experienced before, though it never seemed to work out. Like the time my mom signed me up for a soccer team in fourth grade because of a persuasive flier with a cartoon man and poem that read: Hustle and teamwork will set us apart, talk with your feet, play with your heart, If practice makes perfect then we'll reign supreme, A team above all. Above all, a team! Despite my protests that the team might not be any good and that I had never played soccer before, my mother insisted it wasn't about the soccer, but about learning how to be a team player.

"It turned out she was right. I learned absolutely nothing about soccer. All I learned was which water bottle belonged to which kid on my team so that I could run along the sidelines and hand it to them when they got tired and thirsty. If that isn't teamwork, I don't really know what is. But my mom pulled me off the team after she went to see my third game. She kept saying that I had embarrassed her in front of all the other parents. She confused the hell out of me sometimes, but I tried not to let it get to me. Old ladies are all crazy anyways, and there's really nothing you can do about it. Anyways, my new pattern was going along much better than the soccer team pattern. There were some problems with trying to work out all the getting going to not getting, but that sort of thing wasn't new for me. Things were going pretty okay. There were a few rough spots along the way, of course. For example, Delaney's mother found out that she wasn't going to imaginary tennis because Ellery messed up and forgot to lie. Delaney was pretty angry with him, but I told her that it was her goddamn fault for making him lie in the first place, which was true. I agreed that Ellery was a moron, but it wasn't because of the not-lying. In addition to that, Ellery's highlighter hair started to grow back in, so he bought this stupid woolen hat and started wearing it around everywhere. I asked him why he didn't just leave his appearance alone and be done with it. He kept changing what was is, and it was really getting to me. "Now, instead of a highlighter, I look like a skunk," he told me. "I have to wait three months to change it back to normal, or else it'll all fall out. So now that I've dyed my hair black once, I'll have to dye it black forever unless I want to shave all my hair off or dye it a different color or something..." Ellery trailed off. He seemed very distressed by this.

"Sometimes, being a highlighter isn't so bad," I said. Anyways, just as me, Delaney, and Ellery were getting into a pretty okay routine, something really annoying happened, and it came, like usual, in the form of a person. It was that kid."

I had been putting up with him for almost a whole year. Every other day, he would bring his lunch to the library and sit on the other side of the room, reading books or doing whatever he did. I mostly ignored him before because he was so quiet and pale that you hardly even noticed him. He was one of those people that you eventually tune out, like boring pictures or wallpaper. However, he began moving closer and closer to me. He had stayed in the corner for most of the year, but then he must have worked up his courage one day to move to a table. First, he was four tables away. Then, the very next day, he was three tables away, as though he thought I wouldn't notice. He kept moving his seat every couple of days until he was at the table next to me, practically close enough for me to speak to him. Now, I know you're probably thinking that I'm being stuck-up and antisocial. But it wasn't that I didn't like him or opposed to having him near me. It was the way he was going about it. Every week or so, I'd look up and catch him staring at me. I'm sure he did it more often, too, but he was just very good at hiding it. It wouldn't surprise me if every moment I was trying to read my book or eat my lunch in peace, he was just staring at the top of my head. And then every day, he was closer. It was as though he was sneaking up on me or something. It was driving me crazy.

There was something off about him that I couldn't quite put my finger on. It wasn't a matter of whether he was or wasn't something, but rather a feeling I got when I was around him. He was both more and less than anyone I had ever met. I figured it was because of his constant staring. It seemed like he was working just as hard as I was on trying to move on from something, maybe even harder. I didn't have time for another person with problems to deal with, especially one who might discover the broken windows in my home. I began to believe that all people were crazy and wished I could be a coyote instead. Then, out of nowhere, the kid disappeared. I assumed he had lost interest in bothering me or found somewhere else to eat lunch. But he eventually came back, and I was disappointed that things hadn't stayed the same. It felt like the disappointment of being told it was Christmas Eve and then realizing it wasn't. One day, when I walked into the library, I saw him sitting at the very table I had planned to sit at. I was angry, so I approached him quietly. When I greeted him, he jumped and knocked over his soda and book, making a mess on the table. He tried to pick up his book first and ended up hitting his head on the table.

I walked around the table and placed the soda can upright to prevent any spillage on the library carpet. "You should probably clean that up," I suggested. Without saying a word, the kid reached into his backpack and pulled out napkins from his lunchbox, throwing them onto the spill. "Sorry," he said with a flat tone. I didn't understand why people apologize when they haven't done anything wrong. It's just perplexing. The kid refused to look at me as he continued to toss napkins onto the spill. He obviously felt bad about what had happened. Eventually, after using an excessive number of napkins, he cleaned up the spill and threw them away before sitting back down to read his book. Curious, I asked what he was reading, but couldn't see due to the book being flat on the table. He lifted it up and showed me the cover, and I told him it was a good book. As I stood there, watching him, I wondered about our relationships and if we understood each other.

The kid looked up and said, "I like the Tralfamadorians," with a half-smile. It was obvious that he liked them, and anyone who didn't like them was a fool. Despite his words, I decided to forgive him for whatever he had done to me before and started eating my sandwich. We didn't speak again until the bell rang and he left, leaving me wondering about his age. The next day, I noticed that he had a massive black eye and asked him what happened. He explained that he was in a fight and then shockingly asked if I had any beer. When I said no, he offered to pay for it, but I declined. He went back to reading the same book he had been reading before, leading me to believe that he was a slow reader. I asked him his age, to which he responded with 15. However, he looked much younger than that. His name was Ronny, and he wasn't a part of any gang. The conversation ended with another long silence.

"You shouldn't drink beer," I said. I kind of hated myself for saying it because it wasn't really any of my business, but the thing was, he looked about ten years old. He shrugged. "I don't usually," he said. "I just like to have it." I just kind of stared at him for a while. "Okay," I said. Ronny folded the book face down on the table. "I like the Tralfamadorians, except that they kidnap Billy Pilgrim," he said. "They shouldn't have done that." "No, you don't understand," I said immediately. "It's not like they kidnapped him. It's like they always had kidnapped him, so there wasn't anything any of them could have done about it, so they all just made the best of it and everything." I paused for a second. "And he was happy because he got to have sex with that actress." Ronny sat silently for a while. "But they still shouldn't have done it," he said eventually. There's just no reasoning with some people. "Who did you get into a fight with?" I asked him. He stared at me for a long while. "The other gang," he said eventually. He cracked a smile for the first time. I glared at him. He obviously thought he was very hilarious. "What happened?" I asked him. "We lost," he replied. "It was probably because you were drunk," I said. "That was part of it." "Getting drunk is very bad for your coordination skills." "You're telling me." There was a pause. "You don't like me," he said eventually. He didn't say it like he was mad about it or anything. But I still felt bad because he looked about ten years old. "Nobody likes each other," I told him.

.

"Oh," he said. I could have told him that the reason was because of the different castles, but I didn't know if he would have really understood it very well. "I wish I were in a gang," Ronny said. "Why?" "Because then if I got a black eye, it would be for some sort of reason," he said. "Or, if I were a soldier. Or a Tralfamadorian." "I think you're living in the wrong setting," I said to him. "On multiple levels." I paused thoughtfully. "Tralfamadorians don't like war, though. That's why they skip over them." He obviously wasn't understanding the Tralfamadorians very well. "Yeah," he said finally. I didn't say anything else to Ronny for a couple of days. We just went into the library and sat at the same table, and he was still reading Slaughterhouse Five. He was the slowest reader ever, I swear to God. So things were pretty okay. I was in two different patterns, which was weird for me. I don't know when exactly you get into a pattern with someone, but I guess it's when you expect something from them, and they expect something from you. For example, Delaney and Ellery expected me to be behind the school at 3:30 so that we could drive to the meeting place. And now Ronny expected me to be in the library during lunch periods, and I expected him to be there. And it would be annoying for them if I wasn't, and annoying for me if they weren't. You don't want to get into too many patterns, I guess—they can really turn into a goddamn hassle for everyone involved—but they're okay sometimes. I thought it had something to do with the castles and with the getting going to not getting and back to getting again, but I couldn't completely figure it out. I wanted to ask Ronny, but I was trying to figure out how to say it in terms of the Tralfamadorians. "What's your name?" Ronny asked me one day. I realized I had never told him my name. I didn't know if I was the rude one for not telling him my name or if he was the rude one for not asking me for so long. Things like that can be confusing sometimes.

"I said 'Farley'," I corrected Ronny's confusion as he laughed. "What?" I asked him. "I don't know," he replied, the laughter subsiding. People usually stop laughing if you aren't embarrassed about something. It's just not funny for them anymore. "Are you okay?" I asked him. He stared at me, confused. "What?" "Never mind," I said. "I sometimes have trouble phrasing things properly." Meanwhile, Delaney and Ellery were struggling to recruit people for our club. They couldn't seem to get anyone to join because Delaney kept trying to recruit people she hated and Ellery kept trying to recruit people who hated him. I think Delaney was mostly angry because she wanted to move the boulder, while Ellery just wanted to know how to dress better. He had gotten new glasses, because his mother had finally taken him to an optometrist who concluded that he had the worst eyesight they'd seen in years. "You're going to have to lose the woolen cap, Ellery," Delaney eventually told him. "That, or the glasses. You look like a hipster, and it's an embarrassment to all of us." This upset Ellery, so he decided to take off the woolen hat and put on a baseball cap instead. However, Delaney told him that it looked stupid and didn't match his glasses. So, he got contacts, but they made his eyes water, so he had to go back to glasses. He then decided to cut his hair really short, so only the highlighted parts were showing again. But Delaney told him that it made his glasses look bigger than his head, so he put the woolen hat back on, stopped wearing the glasses, and went around being blind. "Delaney," I interjected eventually, "leave Ellery alone." "I can't help it," she replied. The problem was, she really couldn't. Delaney was a very mean person. I think it was mostly because people kept telling her to fix the rosebushes when she clearly didn't want to. I couldn't decide if she was mean because she didn't fix the rosebushes or if she didn't water them because she was mean. Either way, she wasn't mean because she wanted or had to be, she was just mean because she was mean. Sometimes there's nothing you can do about those kinds of things.

Chapter 11

"It will be fun, I promise," said Ellery, attempting to convince Delaney and me to join his family on a trip to Boston. "I don't want to go to the city," replied Delaney. "My brother was murdered there." "I don't want to go somewhere where I could be murdered," I added. Although I suspected Delaney's claim was false, I didn't want to take any chances. Ellery didn't seem to be deterred. "We're going to a museum," he said excitedly. "My parents said I could bring friends. Besides, Paul will be there." "What museum?" I asked. "We aren't your friends," Delaney interjected. "We hate you." Ignoring us, Ellery continued, "I want you guys to meet Paul. You'll like him." "Just because we're in a club together doesn't mean we're friends," I pointed out. "Farley and I aren't friends." "I don't have any friends," I added. I knew my behavior with the castles had made it difficult for me to make friends. Ellery persisted, "You guys will like Paul. You'll see." "Nobody has any friends," I responded flatly. "My brother was abducted and murdered by a pedophile when he was only five years old," Delaney shared, seemingly enjoying the discomfort in the air. Despite our reservations, Delaney and I went to Boston that weekend to meet Ellery's brother. We had little choice in the matter.

We visited an abstract art museum, and Ellery remarked that Paul had a keen interest in abstract art. I was a bit excited because I had never been to an art museum, taken a painting class, or read a book about art. I thought art could help me to find my motivation whenever I felt lost. However, the abstract artwork had the opposite effect; I left the museum feeling even more confused than when I entered. During the trip, I realized that I despised artwork because it made no sense to me. I understand that you might consider me a hypocrite because I just spoke about senselessness and questioned its existence earlier. However, the abstract art was beyond my understanding and made no sense whatsoever. The artwork displayed at the museum wasn't of anything and consisted of just a bunch of colors thrown together. I felt perplexed and expected to derive some meaning from the chaos that lay before me. The artists seemed either extremely confused or lazy, and their art appeared to be smug. The people observing the artwork were in little groups of two or three and couldn't even look at it effectively by themselves. They would cross their arms and spread their feet apart, tilt their head to the side or wrinkle their foreheads as if they were intently focused on deciphering something meaningful from the abstract painting, which was only a few buckets of paint thrown haphazardly on the canvas. It was as if people were watching each other go into castles that didn't exist. I was frustrated because these people were wasting their time trying to discover some sense where there wasn't any, instead of dealing with their own non-sureness. The fact that they were engrossed in observing each other watch each other was infuriating.

Anyway, Ellery's brother Paul arrived at the art museum an hour late, so Ellery, Delaney, and I sat on a bench surrounded by artwork that didn't interest us. I got up and approached a painting that was mostly gray with a large red splatter in the center. Trying to understand its meaning, I read the caption, which stated that the painting represented the suffering of the Assyrians, Greeks, and Armenians during the Armenian genocide. The artist was inspired by seeing the blood of a young boy after a massacre. I thought that it was more probable that the artist accidentally spilled red paint on a gray canvas and later decided it looked like blood from the genocide. It seemed as if many artists created their work by mistake and then assigned meaning to it afterward. Back on the bench, Delaney appeared suspicious of the artwork, while Ellery was excited for us to meet Paul. He kept standing up and walking in circles around the bench, insisting that Paul was the greatest.

"We know," said Delaney. "I suddenly think our club should be opposed to artwork," I said. Delaney and Ellery both turned to look at me. "You can't do that, Farley," Ellery said, sounding slightly reproachful. "Why not?" I asked. "You can't be opposed to artwork," he whispered. Then he glanced around, as if he were afraid some sort of art Nazi was going to hear us and chase us out of the museum. "Why not?" I asked again. "We're in a society opposed to everything. In case you haven't noticed, artwork is a thing." "Well, yes," Ellery said, rolling his eyes, "But why specifically artwork?" "If this is artwork, then I hate it," I said. "Farley," Delaney said impatiently, "You can't hate artwork." "I hate it," I said, "I goddamn hate it." I didn't like that Delaney was defending the artwork, and I didn't like them telling me what I could or couldn't hate. It just made me hate them and artwork even more. "You mean you don't appreciate it," Ellery corrected me. "Yes," I said. "I don't appreciate it. Just like I don't appreciate you telling me how to feel about artwork." I paused, then folded my arms. "Also, I hate it." Ellery looked downright offended by this point. "But it's artwork," he said angrily. "I know," I replied. "And I hate it." Sometimes, the simplest things are very difficult for people to grasp. "You just can't talk to him, Ellery," Delaney said peevishly. "It's impossible." I wanted to tell Delaney that if she thought I was impossible, she should take a look at herself and stop trying to sell the goddamn castle. If she loved artwork so much, she wouldn't be arguing with me about how much I hated it; she would be looking at it. But she wasn't because the artwork we were surrounded by was the goddamn stupidest thing in the world. Delaney knew it, and Ellery knew it, and all the artists knew it, and all the people here and even the people who owned the museum knew it too. But they were all too goddamn stupid to realize that they knew it. I encountered that sort of problem a lot. "I goddamn hate artwork," I muttered again. They both ignored me this time. "I'm going to the gift shop," Ellery said. "Are you guys coming?"

Neither of us had brought any money, so we couldn't come. Delaney and I sat in silence for a while as we were still angry at each other over the artwork conversation. Eventually, she turned to me and asked, "What would you do if I punched you in the face?" Frowning, I asked, "How hard would you punch me?" Rolling her eyes, she replied, "That's not the point." After a moment's pause, she asked, "As hard as I could." Considering her strength, I said, "I would probably die or get knocked unconscious. It all depends on where you punched me. If it was in the nose, then—" Interrupting me, she said, "No, Farley. I meant if you didn't get knocked unconscious or die or anything, what would you do in retaliation?" Realizing what she meant, I said, "Oh. If I could do whatever I wanted?" Nodding, she waited for my answer. I thought for a moment before saying, "In that case, I would go back in time before you punched me and run away." Seeming angrier than before, she muttered, "Never mind. You're impossible, Farley. This is exactly why nobody wants to join your club." Feeling frustrated, I was about to say something else when Ellery returned with some salt-water taffy. Delaney declined it, and I did too, explaining that I didn't like it. Ellery admitted he didn't either, and Delaney asked why he bought it.

Ellery sighed sadly and said, "I thought you guys would like it," as if it was our fault that we didn't want his salt water taffy. We all sat there in silence for a moment. Then, I decided to take one to prevent it from going to waste. Ellery looked encouraged and handed me a piece. I unwrapped it and threw it at a piece of artwork, which angered Delaney. However, I took another piece and threw it again, and this time it actually stuck to the artwork. Delaney took a piece of salt water taffy, licked it, and stuck it to my forehead, while Ellery laughed. Trying to prove her point, Delaney walked away a few steps and began throwing the candy at my head, instead of the artwork. I complained that she wasn't doing it right and protecting my face with my hands. Meanwhile, Ellery was getting anxious and warned us that we were going to get in trouble.

So, Delaney began throwing pieces of salt water taffy at Ellery instead, clearly enjoying herself. Ellery deserved it for laughing at me and buying the taffy in the first place, so I joined in. Soon enough, it was just the two of us throwing taffy at Ellery, who was trying to shield himself and complaining about our inappropriate behavior in the art museum. That's when we met Paul. At first, we didn't notice him because we were too busy tossing the candy. But when Paul spoke, we stopped. He had been standing there watching us with his arms crossed. And with a furrowed brow, he remarked that it was good to know his brother had matured since he last saw him. Suddenly, Ellery stopped defending himself and turned red. He tried to blame us for our lack of appreciation for artwork. Paul, who walked slowly all the time, stepped closer and complimented Ellery on his hat. This made Ellery even more self-conscious. Finally, he asked Paul if he had seen their parents.

"Yes," Paul said, raising his eyebrows knowingly, "although they're obviously neglecting their babysitting duties." Ellery's face was now even redder, suggesting that things were not going quite as he had hoped. "Paul," he hastily interjected, "these are my friends, Farley and Delaney." Paul stared at us for several moments with his arms crossed and a furrowed brow, making me feel uncomfortable, like a piece of artwork. "Wow," Paul eventually said, "good work, Ellie. You have friends." Delaney suddenly piped up, perhaps in an attempt to get revenge on Ellery for bringing us to the museum, "We aren't his friends. We hate him." It was more likely because she was just a mean person, and sometimes there's nothing you can do about that. "Do you like salt water taffy?" I asked Paul. I didn't want it to go to waste and thought of all the African kids who could benefit from it. If I couldn't cook them rice in my castle, the least I could do was save the salt water taffy from being wasted. Plus, the janitors would have a tough time cleaning it up. This thought made me panic because I didn't have any money to give the janitors as a tip. All I had left was the saltwater taffy, which would be terrible for them to clean up. It was depressing to think of them having to look at the ridiculous abstract artwork museum night after night without even getting tipped. So, I decided that if I earned a trillion dollars, I would buy all the artwork and set it on fire, just so that the poor janitors wouldn't have to look at it day after day.

It seems like good things never happen by accident. For example, when I accidentally threw away money, it just got wasted. But the artwork all looked like terrible accidents; and most of it probably was. However, certain people had decided that it was artwork just because the people who made it were considered artists, which doesn't even mean anything, anyway. As a result, the poor janitors were forced to look at all the stupid accidents of a bunch of idiots and wonder why their accidents didn't get hung up in museums that sell saltwater taffy. It would confuse the hell out of anyone; it had certainly confused the hell out of me, so I couldn't even imagine how it must have been for the janitors. "I am an EMT," Paul was saying. I realized that he was looking at me like I was artwork again, and this made me pretty goddamn angry. "He's alright," Ellery said, although he sounded angrier than ever. "He's not sick or anything. He's just very rude." "I don't know," Paul said scientifically. "He could be having a brain aneurysm." "He's not having a brain aneurysm. He's just having a thought," Delaney said. "It usually happens when he gets bored; I think that the artwork is having an adverse effect on him." She paused. "Either that, or he really doesn't like you." "It's probably the artwork," Ellery said hurriedly, rubbing his neck. I raised my hand and started scratching my head, wondering why they all got so concerned when I wasn't talking, but when I was talking, they barely even listened to me. It was like the people looking at the artwork, I guess. People were always most interested in things that didn't have anything useful to tell them. I had no idea why. I bent down. "We should probably pick up the saltwater taffy," I said to them. After a couple of seconds, I could hear Ellery and Delaney getting down on their knees to help me. However, Paul didn't move; he seemed to still think we were artwork. "Nice friends you've got, Ellie," Paul said eventually. Ellery didn't look up; he was on his hands and knees trying to get a piece of saltwater taffy out from under one of the sculptures. "Yeah," he said without looking up. "They're alright."

Chapter 12

To my great disappointment, we ended up spending the entire afternoon in the art museum. Paul spent about four hours staring at each painting with a serious expression, while Ellery tried to copy him by looking at similar paintings nearby. Delaney and I wandered around aimlessly, feeling increasingly frustrated and depressed as time passed. Delaney repeatedly muttered that she hated Ellery, whether or not he was listening. I considered pointing out how she had defended the artwork earlier, but decided against it because Delaney's anger was unpredictable and sometimes mean. Instead, I kept my mouth shut and tried to avoid further emotional turmoil. However, after Ellery spent an absurd amount of time looking at the same abstract painting, I couldn't resist intervening. I asked him sarcastically if he had found the meaning of life yet, and he responded rudely by telling me to shut up. I didn't listen to him and continued to criticize the painting for being nonsensical and meaningless. Ellery confronted me, and I realized for the first time that he was taller than me.

"I don't care," he snapped. "It doesn't have to mean anything. It's pretty." He balled his hands into fists and momentarily looked as though he would turn back around, but instead he slowly faced me, his expression unfamiliar to me. "You know what your problem is, Farley?" he asked. "No," I replied tentatively, taking a step back from him. He was much taller than me. He spun around and leaned in. "You're always overanalyzing everything," he snapped. "You'd be a lot happier if you weren't always trying to figure everything out. And you'd hate everything less, too," he continued, his voice growing louder to the point where people nearby were staring. He abruptly shifted his attention to Delaney, pointed a finger in her direction, and began berating her. "You don't have to be so mean all the time. You pretend to be nice just so I'll join your stupid club, and then you turn on me and start telling everyone you hate me, and then make fun of my hair and my hat and my glasses and everything..." It dawned on me that Ellery's affection for the painting was likely due to his poor vision. I opened my mouth to share this insight, but Ellery was too far gone in his tirade. "Just because you're meaner than me, that doesn't make you better or smarter," he shouted. "The only reason I became friends with you all was because I thought you'd be different, and different in a good way. But you're worse. You invite me to join your club, but then you lie to me about some list that wasn't even what you said it was. And then you make me look like an idiot in front of my brother and throw things at me and make fun of my glasses..." By this point, Ellery was rubbing his neck and attracting the attention of half the art museum.

"Well, I quit. I don't want to be part of your club anymore," he said angrily before storming out of the gallery, leaving me and Delaney behind wondering what had just happened. Paul, Ellery's brother, just stood there with his arms crossed and a narrowed gaze as if the whole situation was just another piece of art. I thought he was going to follow Ellery since he was his older brother, but he just turned back towards the painting, probably unable to tell the difference. I sighed, realizing that this was why I didn't like getting into patterns because all people are psychotic. "I wish I was a coyote," I told Delaney. "Shut up, Farley," she replied before walking towards another section of the museum. Feeling bad about Ellery's outburst, I decided to go outside and find him. It was raining heavily, but I managed to spot him standing with his arms folded, staring out at the street. I walked up to him and stood there for a moment before saying, "I don't like your brother. He thinks we're all just artwork." Ellery ignored my comment, and I realized that I had said the wrong thing. "You should wear your glasses again," I added. "They make you look stupid, but it's better than acting stupid because you can't see anything."

He still hadn't acknowledged me, and I knew I was just making things worse by talking to him. This was a common occurrence for me, as I tended to say things that didn't make sense to most people. I had learned that most people preferred meaningless paintings to meaningful conversations, and as a result, I struggled to connect with others. As a last resort, I offered Ellery a salt water taffy from my pocket, but he was hesitant to accept it. He expressed his confusion about whether I was mean or just clueless. I explained that we can't help who we are, just as Delaney couldn't help being mean and Ellery couldn't help his bad eyesight. We simply are who we are. Ellery didn't seem convinced, and even mentioned that Delaney had called me psychotic. Despite feeling indignant, I couldn't deny that I often said nonsensical things. However, Ellery seemed to forgive me, and we shared a moment of laughter. I wondered if he truly understood me, or if he was just being polite. Nonetheless, I appreciated his willingness to talk to me and continued trying to connect with others in my own way.

"Uh-huh?" He had already turned to go back into the museum. "Are we planning on leaving soon?" I was worried that another hour in the museum might actually make me psychotic. Ellery gave me a pitying look. "It's too bad you can't appreciate artwork, Farley," he said. I sighed. "It's not that I can't, I just don't. That's all." Ellery gave me a look that was half amused, half annoyed. "Right," he said. He turned around and went back into the museum. I think he probably expected me to follow him, but I didn't. I just stayed out in the rain and waited for him to come back. I wouldn't have cared if the rain had turned into a goddamn hurricane or if a tornado had arrived and started tearing up the buildings. All I cared about was never going into another art museum as long as I lived. It was just too goddamn depressing.

Chapter 13

"I can't believe it," I said. I wasn't trying to be rude, but I couldn't help it. It was getting ridiculous. Ronny glanced up and asked, "What?" I sighed and leaned back in my chair. "I can't believe you're still reading Slaughterhouse Five," I told him. Ronny pushed his hair out of his face. The bruise on his eye had changed colors from black to blue to purple. "So what?" he asked. I stared at him in silence. He went back to his book and I thought our conversation was over. However, a second later, he jumped up, knocking his chair over, and tore the book in half. He ripped out pages and threw them on the table. Then, he balled up the cover and tossed it at my face. "There!" he shouted, his hands shaking with anger. "Are you happy now?" "No," I replied, mostly confused. He stormed out of the library, leaving his backpack and the destroyed book behind. I stared after him, trying to make sense of it all. The librarian came over and gasped, "Farley! What happened?" I told her I didn't know, but that it was the other kid who destroyed the book. She didn't believe me and banned me from the library, threatening to have me suspended for thievery and destruction of school property. I picked up Ronny's backpack and tried to offer it as evidence, but she yelled at me to leave.

So, I grabbed my backpack and left. Sometimes there isn't anything you can do about situations like that. There were still twenty minutes left of lunch, so I decided to wander around the school. It was then that I stumbled upon Ellery and Delaney eating pizza in the hallway. Curious, I asked, "Why are you two eating in the hallway?" Ellery, with his mouth full, replied, "We can't eat in the lunchroom. People will think that we're dating." "Oh," I said, understandingly. There was a brief silence before I revealed, "I have been banned from the library." Delaney burst out laughing. Ellery, who had just swallowed a large bite of his sandwich, asked, "Why?" "It was for thievery and damaging school property, but it wasn't me," I explained. Delaney laughed once more. Ellery looked skeptical. "All right, Farley. Sure, it wasn't you," he remarked, taking another bite of his sandwich. I replied, "He exited through this door about five minutes ago. He's a small kid. You might have seen him." Ellery and Delaney exchanged a glance, and then Delaney skeptically asked, "Are you sure this kid isn't imaginary, Farley?"

I sighed, feeling the weight of the two backpacks on my shoulders causing discomfort. "He's really small," I repeated. "He looks about ten years old, but he's actually fifteen. His hair is too long and messy, and he's got a huge bruise over his eye." Both Ellery and Delaney stared at me. "Haven't seen him," Ellery replied. "Sorry, Farley," Delaney added, "I think this kid might be your hallucination." I held out the backpack towards them. "This is his," I said, trying to prove my point. There was a pause before Ellery spoke up. "Farley, have you been stealing things again?" He grinned stupidly, making me think he had been hanging out with Delaney too much. I turned and walked away, frustrated with their lack of help. I needed to find Ronny and return his backpack so he could vindicate me and get me back into the library. But Ronny was nowhere to be found during the rest of lunch period. Just as I was about to give up and throw his backpack in the dumpster, I spotted him outside the janitor's closet, staring at a can of coke. I dropped his backpack in his lap, causing him to flinch from the weight. He didn't seem to care though, continuing to stare ahead. "You left your backpack in the library," I said bluntly. Ronny turned his head to me. "Shouldn't you be getting to class?" he asked. I gestured towards him. "Shouldn't you?" "Nobody comes looking for you down here," he replied cryptically. "Well, that's great, but you need to talk to the librarian because you've gotten me expelled from the library," I explained, unable to contain my frustration.

He scratched his head and said, "Oh." I crossed my arms and snapped, "Oh? Is that all you've got to say for yourself? We don't all have janitor closets we can go and hide in, you know." "I'm not hiding," he replied. "I'm visiting Steve." "Steve?" I asked, irritated. Suddenly, a middle-aged guy with wispy hair and a poking out belly came out of the janitor's closet.

He was holding both of his hands behind his back. "Is he with you?" the janitor asked Ronny in a gruff, dull-sounding kind of voice. Ronny shrugged and then nodded. Just as I was about to protest, the janitor Steve took out his hands from behind his back and offered me a coke. I declined, which seemed to irritate him. Steve went back inside the closet, while Ronny and I sat outside. I asked Steve if he ever finds money accidentally thrown in the trash, which he denied. Steve tried to explain to me that it's impossible to find something without looking for it. I felt depressed that they didn't even try to find money in the trash. Steve sensed my sadness and said he sometimes finds money on the floor. I snapped, "Well, that doesn't goddamn count, does it? That could happen to anyone!" Steve shrugged and went back inside the closet. I sat beside Ronny and put my head in my hands. Ronny asked if anything was wrong.

"I am having some problems with my castle," I said. "You wouldn't understand." Ronny didn't seem to know how to respond, so he took a sip of his coke instead. Eventually, he let out a sigh and asked if I wanted to leave. I agreed and he stood up, but I clarified that I meant my statement in an intellectual sense. He rolled his eyes and walked away, but I followed him anyway. I wanted to break my routine and make my classmates wonder where I was. On our way out, I asked Ronny if we were going to get in trouble for truancy, but he called me "retarded" for even suggesting it. As we walked, I complained that Delaney had been driving me everywhere and I wasn't used to walking anymore. Ronny offered to leave me behind, but I asked how far we had to go. When he said it was about a mile, I decided to come along.

Chapter 14

So, I began walking again and we walked in silence for a while. I wasn't paying much attention to our destination since it's not one of my strong points. My mind was preoccupied with the janitor and I was contemplating different ways I could get inside his castle, but none seemed practical. It didn't make sense for him to collect change from the garbage cans, but I wanted him to do it. I realized that most things that seemed sensible were actually nonsensical. Therefore, something that didn't make sense could actually make sense. I wished I could explain this to the janitor so he could understand. Suddenly, Ronny snapped me out of my thoughts and inquired about where I was going. I realized that he had turned down a driveway, and I had kept walking down the road. I apologized and followed him up his driveway, which was less steep than Delaney's but longer and winding, surrounded by dense woods. We entered Ronny's house, which appeared smaller in comparison to the towering trees. Ronny switched on an old television but muted the sound. I asked him, "What's the point of that?" Ronny snapped at me, irritated, as if he had forgotten about my presence and was annoyed that I interrupted him. "It's my house, isn't it?"

After a moment, he snapped. I agreed that it was indeed his house, and then he seated himself on one of the stools situated at his counter since there was no dining table. Although I wasn't particularly engrossed in his kitchen, I observed a vast collection of books in the next room. Therefore, I turned and headed in that direction. To my dismay, the entire bookshelf appeared to be filled with different religious texts or yoga-related books, neither of which attracted my attention. Ronny's voice echoed through the doorway, "You know, it's impolite to rummage through other people's possessions." I spun around and saw him standing a few feet behind me. "So," I continued, "I assume your parents are Buddhist, Hindu, Muslim, Scientologists, or something like that?" I pivoted back to the bookshelf and added, "Or perhaps all of the above?" Ronny's eyes narrowed, and he folded his arms across his chest, resembling a frustrated child whose toys are being investigated. "My father is a religious scholar," he stated indignantly. "That makes sense," I replied. "What about your mother? Is she a yoga instructor?" "No," Ronny snapped, growing more irritated by the second. "They merely enjoy practicing yoga." "Ah," I said. "Did they meet through yoga?" "No," Ronny snapped once more. "Do you want to leave that area, maybe? I didn't permit you to go in there, you know." "You didn't tell me not to," I reminded him as I trailed behind him out of the room. "You're going to mess everything up," Ronny complained. "Then it will be blamed on me."

"I'm sorry," I said. "Are your parents here now?" Ronny laughed and walked over to the fridge. "No, they're traveling," he replied. "For how long?" I asked. "Oh, I don't remember," he said dismissively. "So, are you here... alone?" My curiosity and jealousy mixed together. "Well, Sam comes around every now and again," he shrugged and changed the television channel to boxing. As one of the men took a hard blow to the face, Ronny winced and looked away. "Who's Sam?" I asked. "My uncle," Ronny replied. "I don't know where he is right now, but he's a pretty cool guy. You should see the stuff he gives me." He grinned wickedly and offered me a beer. "I thought we talked about this," I scolded him as he took a can from the fridge. "What would the Tralfamadorians think, Ronny?" The smile disappeared from his face. "Fuck the Tralfamadorians," he snapped. "They're useless." "Well," I said as he sat down next to me and took a sip of his becr, "they're fictional, Ronny. They're only as useful as you make them." He glared at me. "You're just jealous because your uncle doesn't bring you beer." "No, I'm not," I said. Ronny ignored me and took another drink. "You know what your problem is, Farley?" he said. "I'd like to," I replied. He shot me an irritated look before continuing. "I've met a lot of people like you," he said.

"Really?" I asked. It wasn't something I heard often. "Not exactly like you," Ronny muttered, "but with a similar problem." "What's that?" I asked. He took another long swig, then put the bottle down on the table. He seemed like he was going to take a break, but then changed his mind and took a small sip followed by a larger one. Then he hiccupped rather loudly and said, "Well, you're very intellectually unhappy." "Oh," I said, watching him take another drink. "I guess so." "That's not your problem, though," he said. "What is it?" I asked, feeling annoyed. He took a long sip and said, "You like it." "Like what?" I asked confusedly. "Your intellectual unhappiness," he replied. He got off the stool and started walking around the room with the beer in his hand. "You think it makes you a martyr or something. But you've got to realize," he paused, then finished off the beer in a large gulp. He tossed it onto a nearby chair. "You've got to realize that it doesn't make you a martyr." He turned around and went to the fridge, taking out two beers this time. He tried to slide one over to me, but it toppled over and I had to catch it to prevent it from falling. "What does it make me?" I asked him. He popped the can open and took a long, thoughtful sip. "At the end of the day," he said eventually, "it just makes you unhappy." "Oh," I said. I stared at the can in my hands and put it on the table as it was making my fingers cold. "What should I do, then?" I asked him. Ronny didn't say anything for a while; he just sat there, sipping his beer. Eventually, however, his sips got longer and turned into chugging. Then he turned the can upside down and tilted his head back, causing the beer to spill down his chin, neck, and onto the front of his shirt. When he finished, he threw the can at the wall, but not out of anger, rather out of jubilation. He wiped his chin, turned around, and said, "If it were me, I'd try whatever I could to make myself happy." Things became strange after that; Ronny went to the fridge for a third beer, and I said, "Ronny, don't you think that's too much for such a short amount of time?" He turned towards me and said, "My uncle Sam brought over a ton," as if quantity was the only issue.

"I told him, 'You look like you're about ten years old,' and he sighed, staring at a vacant spot in the corner of the fridge. 'My uncle doesn't bring over much food,' he said. 'Well,' I replied, 'that's not good.' Ronny kept staring at the fridge and explained, 'I guess it's not that he wouldn't bring it. I just don't ask for it as much. He always brings over blueberries because of their antioxidants.' 'Okay,' I said. Ronny opened his third beer of the afternoon and sat on the couch. 'I finished Slaughterhouse Five years ago, but I just like it,' he said. 'My uncle is really a good guy,' he told me. 'I'm sure he is,' I replied. Ronny then said, 'He's really a good guy. He's not my whole uncle, though. He's my half-uncle. He's only twenty-five, and he's still a lot of fun. He knows I feel bad a lot, so he wants me to get as happy as possible.' 'That makes sense,' I said. Suddenly, Ronny snapped and said, 'I can tell what you're thinking, though. You don't like him.' 'I wasn't thinking that,' I lied, realizing that Ronny was the type of person you couldn't lie to. He persisted, 'I can tell you don't like him.' Finally, I admitted, 'Well, no one likes anyone.' Ronny sank onto the couch and said slowly, 'I suppose you're right. Why is that?' I replied, 'It's because of the castles. Nobody can get into each other's castles.' Ronny took another sip and muttered, 'That's a shame.' 'It is,' I said. 'It's a real shame. I've been trying to figure it out by forming patterns with people, but it hasn't helped at all.'"

"It's no use," Ronny said. "Most people don't want to form patterns with you. They just want to be able to say they've formed patterns with you." I was impressed with his insight and told him that's how my mother is. She doesn't want to watch me cook rice for African kids in my castle. She wants to watch other people watch me cook rice for African kids in my castle. Ronny looked confused for a moment, but then laughed and asked why I would cook rice for African kids. I explained that they can't cook their own rice in Africa and that's why they're so skinny. I thought I would cook all their rice for them if I could get them into my castle. Ronny laughed and pointed out that African people don't just eat rice. I realized that I had only had a vague idea without fully understanding it and felt guilty. Meanwhile, Ronny was laughing so hard that he spilled his beer on his stomach. I, on the other hand, was having a terrible day because I had been banned from the library, had issues with the quarters and Steve the janitor, and had just realized that I had no idea how to properly feed all the African kids in my castle.

I glared at Ronny for a few moments, seething with anger. He eventually stopped laughing, sat up, and gulped down whatever beer hadn't spilled onto his shirt. Despite the situation, he still had a grin on his face. "Hey, you know what Sam told me once?" he asked me. I replied despondently, "What?" For no particular reason, Ronny threw the empty beer can at me. I didn't bother trying to catch it, but he missed the target by a wide margin, and the can hit the table before rolling under a nearby chair. "He said, 'nothing's ever funnier than unhappiness.' I'm starting to get what he meant," Ronny chuckled. I snapped, "Samuel Beckett said that!" He took a few moments to stop laughing before responding with, "So what? Just because someone famous said it doesn't mean nobody else can say it again." Despite being angry, I began to understand why Ellery laughed at my "castle." Ronny's words made me ponder if trying to be happy was futile since nobody else would come into my life other than to mock me. I grabbed the beer can from the table, determined to salvage my pride. This act was symbolic of slamming the doors of my hypothetical castle in the faces of everyone who had ever mistreated me. Ronny interrupted my thoughts, "Wow, Farley, you're drinking fast." Realizing how quickly I had consumed the beer, I muttered, "This tastes awful." Despite the bad taste, I continued to drink it. Most things in life were similar to climbing a hill - unpleasant at first, but you kept going anyhow, for no logical reason. I didn't want to spill any on my shirt, so I drank the beer slowly at a 100-degree angle. When I finally finished, I slammed the can on the table like Ronny did earlier. "I'm not happy yet," I told Ronny. A slight dizziness and nausea were the only things I felt. "Try another," he replied.

"I did it. It tasted just as bad as the first one and made me feel even dizzier, increasing my nausea. Furious, I turned and threw the empty can against the wall. "I'm still not happy!" I shouted at Ronny. He looked at me thoughtfully and said, "That's strange." I retorted, "Yeah, it's damn weird!" He suggested I have another can, but I refused, declaring that his advice was useless. I walked towards the couch, almost tripping over one of the empty cans on the way there, and sat down next to him. As I stared at the table, Ronny commented, "Maybe you're the problem, not my advice. Perhaps you don't want to be happy." I replied, "It's asking too much to want to be happy. I just want to feel happy." Ronny hiccupped again and stood up. "You know," he said, "The issue is you were drinking the wrong stuff. I have some high-quality products in my basement."

"Why the hell was I drinking the low-quality stuff in the first place?" I snapped, exasperated. "Sorry," he said, shuffling away from the couch. "I'll get it." Meanwhile, my mind wandered off to my mother and her book club. I envisioned myself barging in, and my mother asking me how my day had been, and me simply staring at her and then vomiting on her shoes. The idea made me chuckle lightly, but it still didn't make me feel any happier. Ronny appeared again with about six or seven bottles. I burst out laughing at the sight of him, as he still looked like a ten-year-old and was staggering around in an amusing manner, with liquid splashed all down his face and shirt, and hair wet and clinging around his neck. "What's so funny?" he asked, a silly grin spreading across his face and I laughed even harder. "Hey, what's funny?" he repeated, but just as he spoke, he lost his balance, tripped forwards, and dropped all of the bottles on the floor. To my surprise, none of them shattered. As I watched him, helpless on the floor, looking bewildered, I laughed even harder. One of the bottles rolled over to me, and I asked, "Can I have this?" Ronny's expression turned alarmed, and he quickly grabbed the bottle out of my hand. "No, not that one," he said nervously, then rolled another bottle towards me. "I can't goddamn open it," I snapped at him.

He searched around in his pocket for approximately two hours before finally producing a bottle opener and tossing it to me. It took some time for me to figure out how to use it, but once I managed to pry off the top, I gulped down the contents as fast as I could. I hoped that this drink would make me happy, or else I would have gone home and vomited on my mother's footwear instead. Ronny leisurely called out, "Does it taste any better?" I didn't reply, but the drink did have a slightly improved flavor. Regardless, I continued to chug it down. I compared it to climbing up a hill - once I reached the top, I just let it all spill out. "I feel slightly happier now," I stated, unsure if the drinks were actually responsible or if I just wanted to feel that way. "I should have another one of those, Ronny." "Do you know what time it is?" he suddenly inquired, ignoring my comment. "I'm not sure, two maybe?" I guessed. "It's three-thirty," Ronny dramatically announced. "Oh." I realized my phone had been left on the table and stumbled over to it, feeling more stable than normal yet simultaneously less secure. My phone display showed two missed calls from Delaney, which brought me a great deal of joy. "You have another one?" I asked Ronny, concluding that the alcohol brought out my happiness. He stood up and handed me a bottle. "Are you happy now?" he questioned. "I don't care," I replied. We eventually lost count of how many bottles we had emptied and, after a while, the world seemed incredibly amusing to us. "Farley," Ronny solemnly stated when we were both collapsed on the sofa, "It's a pity that nobody can like each other." "It doesn't matter," I laughed, which felt odd and yet perfectly fitting given the hysterical situation. My sight had begun to blur, similar to when you try on someone else's glasses and struggle to focus on anything. "You know what, Ronny?" I asked. "What?"

"We're drunk," I stated with certainty, finding the situation highly amusing. Ronny seemed surprised and thought he was just very hydrated. I corrected him, but my mind was too scattered to focus, and I suggested he meet my friends. I dialed Delaney's number, trying to put her on speaker but accidentally muting her instead. After I finally got her on speaker, I informed her I was drunk, which caused Ellery to ask if it was true. Delaney demanded to know where we were and why we were drunk, and I asked her to pick us up in a desperate situation. When asked who I meant, I replied with a joke that Ronny and I found hilarious, even though it didn't make sense.

"I turned to Ronny and demanded, 'What is your address?' I put him on speakerphone so Delaney could hear him tell us where he lived. Ronny yawned and introduced himself to Delaney, but I reminded him to give his address. We laughed at his mistake. Delaney became annoyed when Ronny asked if she was picking him up too, not realizing he lived with us. I felt guilty when he sounded disappointed, so I offered to abduct him into our society. Ronny went to pack, and I dozed off. When I woke up, he had a huge bag and seemed concerned I was dead. He shared his belief that God and the Tralfamadorians work together, killing people when they figure everything out."

I asked him if I would live forever if I never figured it out. Ronny said no and explained that the person who knows the answer may kill those who figured it out or those who will never figure it out. He advised me to make it seem like I'm about to figure it out to survive longer. I asked if he learned this from his parents, but he said he learned it on his own. I asked what happens after one die, and he said the earth eats you. I asked if anything happens after figuring it out, but he said that the purpose is for someone else to figure it out once you're gone. I asked about the end of the world, but he said it wouldn't matter as they would have already figured everything out. Suddenly, there was knocking on the door, making Ronny anxious until I reminded him of our planned road trip.

"Oh," he said, looking considerably relieved. "Right." I stumbled over to the door and swung it open. Delaney was standing there with her arms folded, her attempt at disapproval being trumped by triumphant amusement and mockery. Ellery stood behind her looking slightly nervous and very excited. "Oh, hello!" I said gleefully. "Hey, Ronny! Are you ready for the road trip?" Delaney snorted in amusement. "What road trip?" "The, you know," I sighed. "Ronny!" Ronny stumbled towards the door, the bag still around his neck. "Oh, hello there! Are you Farley's not-friends?" "That's exactly what we are," Delaney said. "I suppose you're his imaginary friend?" "Oh, yes," Ronny replied, nodding affirmatively. "I've spent most of my life as an imaginary friend, actually." "Excellent," Delaney said briskly. "Well, Farley, if you want, Ellery and I can drive you to the meeting place, so you don't have to go home and tell your mother you've been drinking." I blinked several times. "But I want to tell her!" I shouted. "She'll be so proud of me!" "Ellery, can you take him to the car?" Delaney said, rudely discounting my opinion. Ellery stepped forward and grabbed my arm, but made no attempt to move me. Delaney then turned towards Ronny, who was standing in the doorway and staring at her with wide eyes. She eyed him disapprovingly. "How old are you, twelve?" "I'm nine hundred years old," he said gravely, "like Methuselah. It's taking me a while to figure things out." "Of course, you are," she said briskly. "Well, I suppose you're coming with us?" Ronny nodded solemnly, then outstretched his hand. "It's nice to meet you," he said, his wide eyes fixated on her face. "You have wonderful eyelids. They're very…white. You know what? We're all white. Isn't that weird? All of the Tralfamadorians are green, I think."

"Right," repeated Delaney. "Ellery?" Ellery pulled me towards the car, and I stumbled along behind him. We stopped at the car, and he looked me up and down. "Jesus Christ, Farley," he said. "I have motion sickness," I informed him. Wordlessly, he opened the front door. I grabbed onto the headrest and pulled myself in. I couldn't find the seatbelt, so I lied back and closed my eyes. I vaguely heard Ronny Orwell follow Delaney into the car and Delaney asking, "Where the hell are your parents, kid?" "They're trying to figure it out," he said. "But they suck at it." I heard Delaney sigh. "Ellery, can you pull him in?" "Why are we taking him?" Ellery asked nervously. "We don't even know him." "He's coming!" I shouted angrily. "I inducted him into our society!" "God damn it, Farley," Delaney snapped. "You can't just induct whoever you like into the society, especially twelve-year-old." "He's fifteen," I explained. "I'M NINE HUNDRED YEARS OLD!" Ronny shouted from behind me. "Just get in," Delaney grumbled. I heard some sort of struggle before a car door slammed. I opened my eyes as Delaney got into the seat next to me. "Well, Farley," she said, sighing. "I have to say I'm disappointed." "For getting drunk?" I asked her. The car suddenly jerked backward before speeding forward, making my stomach lurch, but I decided not to mention it. "For getting drunk without me," she snapped. "Oh," I said. "Did you want to be drunk too?"

"No," she said, "but I'm horrified that I almost missed something so incredibly amusing." "Oh," I said, "sorry." We drove in silence for some time, except for Ronny hiccupping every couple of minutes in the back seat. Eventually, Ellery spoke up. "We're going to get in trouble." "Shut the hell up, Ellery," Delaney and I said. My speech was a bit muffled and slower, but I meant the same thing as Delaney. Delaney continued, "This is the first amusing thing that has happened in ages. Don't ruin it." "Yeah, Ellery," I echoed, "Don't ruin it." "You guys," Ronny said from the back seat, "Don't worry. I have a ton of good beer in my bag." At this point, Ellery completely lost his head. He started shouting at me and Delaney to pull over immediately because we were going to get arrested for driving under the influence of alcohol. Delaney tried to explain to him that we weren't driving under the influence, but Ellery wouldn't listen. He was convinced he was going to jail and ruin his chances of getting into Princeton. Then he tried to tackle Ronny and take the bag away from him. Ronny responded with surprising violence, and Delaney had to shout at both of them to quiet down or else she would turn the car around. When they didn't listen, she slammed on the brakes, causing both of them to smash their heads into the front seats, and me to almost fall forward through the windshield since I couldn't find my seatbelt. After that, both of them seemed to calm down, but Ronny was clutching the bag defensively, and Ellery was muttering something under his breath. Although Delaney's abrupt maneuver had successfully stopped the fight in the back, my motion sickness didn't bode well. I tried to hold it in, but eventually said, "Delaney, I'm going to puke."

She abruptly hit the brakes at the top of the hill, leaned over me, threw open the door, and unceremoniously pushed me out of the car. I tumbled on the ground and rested my cheek on the pavement. "Ah," I sighed, "I feel better now." "You're such an idiot, Farley," Delaney barked, more concerned about her car than me. "You're right, I admit it," I replied with my face still on the ground. "Get back in or I'm leaving you behind," she snapped. "You moronic fool." At that moment, my stomach felt queasy again, but I tried to ignore it and sang a song instead. I found it hilarious and burst into laughter again. "Farley!" Delaney yelled. "Are you coming or not?" I turned over, faced the side of the road, and threw up. "Perfect," Delaney sighed. "I'm parking the car in the garage before anyone else loses their lunch. You two," she pointed at Ellery and Ronny, "get out." As they exited the car, Ellery cursed quietly, and Ronny sang a silly song loudly. Ellery eventually told him to be quiet, but Ronny retaliated by mentioning his ugly hat.

Chapter 15

"Ellery, it's a once-in-a-lifetime opportunity," Delaney said excitedly, addressing Ellery's concerns. I sat on a tree stump, watching as Delaney tried to convince Ellery to join us. "Tell your parents you're staying over at a friend's house. You can still go to school tomorrow and if you miss a day, just say you weren't feeling well. I'll drive you home," Delaney continued persuading Ellery. Ellery looked hesitant, stating that his parents would wonder where he was if they had not met his friend's parents. I walked over, put my hand on Delaney's shoulder, and asked what was going on. Delaney pushed me away, disgusted by my breath that smelled like vomit and her meanness. I fell back and saw Ronny sitting on one of the tree stumps blankly staring into space. Delaney explained that we could have a lot of fun spending the night there, pointing at Ronny who had lined up bottles in a strange shape. Ronny said he hoped to signal the Tralfamadorians. Ellery protestingly cried out that this was what bad people do, and we'll ruin our brains. He further said that he had learned about it all in health class and drew reference from his brother Paul.

"I have an idea," Delaney said, a wicked grin spread across her face. "Let's make Ellery our project. We'll teach him how to be cooler, and then he can finally make some real friends. What do you say, guys?" I rolled my eyes, not really in the mood for this nonsense. Ronny shrugged in agreement, but I could tell he wasn't particularly invested either way. "Fine," I said half-heartedly, knowing there was no point in arguing. "Let's make Ellery cool." As the four of us walked away, leaving Ellery alone on the tree stump, I couldn't help but feel a twinge of guilt. But it wasn't like we were really doing anything mean to him, right? We were just trying to help him fit in. Or at least, that's what I told myself.

"Okay," Delaney said, "here's what we need to do." She paused, then glanced at Ellery and Ronny. Ellery was still staring at the ground and Ronny was busy organizing the bottles. "Hey, you two, pay attention, why don't you?" Both of their heads snapped towards her. Her smile widened.

"Alright," she said. First, Delaney helped Ellery stumble through a call to his parents. I don't remember exactly what the story was, but I do remember Ellery giving mono-syllabic answers and Delaney doing the majority of the talking. The strange smile persevered on her face. It was beginning to feel rather unsettling watching her. It was as if she were a Cheshire cat coaxing a fly to drown itself in a puddle. Finally, she hung up the phone. "There," she said to Ellery, "looks like your parents aren't quite as concerned about your safety as you thought they were." Ellery said nothing. Next, I took out my phone to call my mother. I knew it was necessary because she would eventually become concerned about my whereabouts once the book club had left and she realized that there was an extra portion of casserole left over. But I was rather disappointed that I wouldn't have the opportunity to puke on her shoes. I knew that it was rude, but I desperately wanted to. I had fantasized about it happening three or four times already since the thought had first occurred to me, and it was really going to be a big letdown now that it wasn't going to happen. "No, no, no," Delaney snapped. "You are not going to be doing the talking, Farley. You're the worst liar I've met in my entire life, and you're drunk." "My mom doesn't pay very good attention," I told her. "She's very focused on watching other people watch the castles." "Just be quiet," she snapped and dialed the number herself. My mother answered on the third ring. "Hello?" she inquired. "Hello, Mrs. Underwood," Delaney said in that very sweet kind of voice that girls can put on. "My name is Marcia Owens. Farley's going to be staying over at my house tonight. We need to work on a group project for our biology class, and it's going to take all night to finish."

"Oh, biology class?" my mother asked loudly, as I could hear the book club laughing in the background. "How fascinating!" "Hi, Mom!" I shouted into the phone. "What are you all reading?" Delaney snatched the phone away from me, covering it with her hand and giving me a menacing stare. "Hello, Farley!" my mother yelled back, her voice almost as bold as mine. "You sound like you're having fun!" "Excellent fun!" I shouted back. "Wonderful!" she exclaimed. "Are you with your girlfriend, Farley?" she asked in the same voice. However, before I could respond, she continued, "Well, it's excellent that you're so dedicated to your schoolwork. You kids have a good time, all right?" "Goodbye, Mrs. Underwood," Delaney interrupted hastily, hanging up the phone as quickly as she could. She breathed a sigh of relief and then directed her frustration at me. "You're lucky your mother is clueless," she snapped. "She's not really clueless," I replied cheerfully. "She's just smart enough to know that being clueless makes her happy." Delaney shot me an exasperated look and then threw my phone back at me. She turned away and began chatting with Ellery, but my mind was elsewhere. I kept thinking about how I was going to stumble home the next day and vomit all over my mother's shoes. It didn't matter if I was still drunk by then – I was going to do it anyway. The next thing I knew, Delaney was gone. I glanced around for her, but Ellery and Ronny were the only ones nearby. Ronny was still fiddling with the beer bottles, and Ellery was twisting his hat in his hands, his vibrant blond hair starting to grow back. He put on his glasses and then slipped the hat into his pocket. "Where's Delaney?" I asked him. Ellery took the hat out of his pocket and gazed at it mournfully for a few seconds before standing up and frantically pacing around. "Hey, Ellery," I said impatiently. He turned to face me. "Where's Delaney?" He shrugged slightly. "She went to... move her car. To the other side of the woods. So, we can, you know, leave without her mom..." he trailed off, looking at Ronny. Ronny was still playing with the bottles. I'm not sure how long Ellery stood there staring at him, but suddenly he lunged forward, pushed Ronny to the ground, and snatched one of the bottles.

"What the hell, man," Ronny mumbled, now lying upside down on the forest floor. "You've ruined it. I would've given you one if you'd asked for it." Ellery opened the beer and took a very small sip. He spat it out on the ground. "There's sand in here, you idiot!" he snapped. "It's a flavor enhancer," Ronny said, rolling his eyes. "If you don't want it, give it back." Ellery turned away and took another sip, grimacing as he did so. "I hate you all," he mumbled. Then he wandered off into the woods in the direction of where Delaney was supposedly moving her car. I pushed myself to my feet. I had begun to feel bad again, and I didn't like it very much. "Give me another one," I said to Ronny. "It's starting to wear off already." He opened one for me, and then misguidedly attempted to toss it to me, resulting in me spilling a good portion of it down my front. "What in the hell did you do that for?" I spat at him. "My bad," he yawned. "Farley? You're not-friends are mean." "Everyone's mean," I said. Then I frowned. "There is sand in here." "It's a flavor enhancer," Ronny said, rolling his eyes. "They're Sam's. That's why the tops have already been opened. See? He's going to be mad that we're drinking them all. I was supposed to wait till he got back." "Well, just get some other beer and put sand in it," I said. We were sitting there drinking the sand-beer until Delaney and Ellery walked back. Ellery's bottle was nearly empty by this point, and he was looking extremely angry about it. "Ellery," I called to him. "You know what it is? Nobody takes the proper things seriously anymore." Wordlessly, he walked over to Delaney and handed her one of the bottles. "Your turn," he said. "It's the worst shit imaginable." I didn't pay much attention to them after that. I was far too interested in my own sand-beer. Everything had started to feel hilarious again, so I got myself to thinking about what does or doesn't make people. I was wondering if drinking beer made you feel more or less than you already were. I couldn't decide. I was hoping that things would go back to being normal in the morning, but then again, maybe I was also hoping that they wouldn't, because then I might die like Ronny had said. I didn't feel like I wanted to die before things went back to being normal, but then again, maybe that was the whole point in the first place. I was pulled out of my thoughts when there seemed to be some sort of commotion. I narrowed my eyes and noticed that Delaney was sitting next to Ellery and clapping rather sarcastically as he finished off a bottle. "I'm impressed, Ellery," Delaney said. "I didn't think you'd be able to drink three of them."

"I really hate this," Ellery said, but at this point, he had a silly smile on his face and was laughing with Delaney. "How much have you had anyway?" "Just a couple sips," Delaney replied. "I just wanted to watch everyone get drunk for the entertainment value." She gave Ellery the same smile. For a moment, I thought Ellery had frozen up again. His face abruptly hardened, and I wondered if his blood had thickened and he would become like one of the trees - a statue. But after a strange pause, he erupted. "You goddamn bitch!" I was hit with a wave of panic as Ellery lunged at Delaney, knocking her out of her seat. His hands were moving up and down like levers, blurring and changing. I kept shouting at Ellery to stop, trying to intervene, but he turned on me and started hitting me instead. I covered my head and began shouting about castles and janitors. Suddenly, there was a tinkling sound, and Ellery let out a soft moan, rolling off of me. Delaney was standing there holding the broken top of a beer glass. The earlier expression had left her face, replaced by a silent panic I'd never seen before. She turned to Ellery and said, "I'm sorry." Her words were sincere, and I almost didn't recognize her voice. Ellery whispered, "Please, I just wanted everyone to stop staring at me." Delaney picked up her beer and stood it upright to prevent it from spilling. "It's almost all spilled anyway," she said to Ellery. Ellery didn't respond. Delaney took another sip of her beer and made a face. "Now there's dirt in it too." "It was already sandy," I said, yawning. "Hey Ronny, are you alive?" "I think so," Ronny replied slowly. "Are you?" "I haven't figured it out yet," I said, feeling extremely dizzy and tired. "That's good. Hey, Farley?" "Yeah?" I asked, yawning again. "If you figure it out, will you promise to tell me?" "Of course," I replied. "But I'll probably be dead." "Tell me anyway. I'll follow you, just tell me."

"What are you two talking about?" demanded Delaney. She had finished her original bottle and was now pushing Ronny out of the way in search of another. "You can't be in a castle if you aren't in it!" I shouted, unsure of who I was speaking to. "You can't find something you're not looking for!" Delaney walked over to me and stood over me, appearing to have returned to normal. She gave me a muted smile, kind yet not very kind at all. "Don't be an idiot, Farley," she said. "That's the only time you'll ever find anything, anything that's worth finding anyways." She chuckled at my stupidity for several moments, then went to sit next to Ellery. "Oh, of course," I said dreamily. Ronny called out that he had a confession to make, but nobody was listening to him. I closed my eyes and leaned my head back, worried that I was going to fall over and chuckling to myself. Suddenly, I realized it was dark out. "What time is it?" I called to Ronny, but nobody answered. "It's goddamn I, Farley," Ronny called to me. "It's

IOL, okay?" I heard giggling from somewhere left of me that sounded strange and distorted, frightening me even though I knew it was Ellery.

"You're looking at that upside down, kid," he said, gleefully. "Hey Delaney, I think you should have one more...okay?" The laughing started up again and it felt like my hands were starting to tremble. I was a bit worried about the laughing because you never knew what it might mean. Nobody could ever take the proper things seriously anymore, especially not Ellery. "Get away from my castle, Ellery!" I shouted angrily. Even as I was saying it, the words were coming out strangely, like they were being put through a wind tunnel. I started to panic all of a sudden; I got to my feet and started walking up and down. It didn't feel like I was dizzy anymore, but I felt very unstable all the same. I noticed that Ellery was still lying on his side and laughing. I crouched next to him and bent very close to his face. "What's so funny?" I asked him. "This hat," he muttered. "I think it's trying to kill me." I frowned. The hat lay several feet away and looked relatively harmless to me. "Why are you laughing then?" I asked him. "Never show fear, Farley," he whispered. "You can't ever show the hat fear. Okay?" I blinked and shook my head before I realized that the hat was kind of glowing slightly. "Oh," I said. "You two are freaking weird," Delaney said. She was the only one who was still drinking; Ronny looked like he had fallen asleep across the clearing. However, I couldn't really tell because his back was to us. I began to panic and started walking towards him. "Ronny?" I asked. "Are you alright?" I went over to him and turned him over. He was staring at me with wide eyes and panting heavily. "I shouldn't have taken them," he panted, his hands shaking. "Taken what?" "Sam said not to drink them without him there..." Ronny hissed. "Farley...Farley, listen..." "What?" "I think I might be dying," he hissed. "Why?" I demanded.

"I admit, it's because of the uncooked rice," he said. "We're all really dying because of the uncooked rice, Farley, if you think about it." I thought for a moment before responding. "No, we're not," I said. "It's true," Ronny gasped. "God is bad at managing rice. He only gives it to certain people in certain areas and ignores everyone else." "Oh," I replied, noticing the size of Ronny's eyes. "Your eyes are huge." "That's because God spends all his time with the Tralfamadorians. He loves them and they're higher quality than us. I wish I was one of them," Ronny said, his eyes growing larger. "I know, Ronny," I replied in a kind but somewhat patronizing voice. "He's terrible at rice management," Ronny continued. "He gives a lot to some people and none to others." "Why doesn't he work on it then?" I asked. "It's important." "I don't know if you've noticed, Farley," Ronny said, "but God is kind of a douchebag." "I have noticed, but why?" I pressed. "Sometimes things just are," Ronny replied slowly. I couldn't believe what I was hearing. "Wow," I said, "what time is it?" "Did you hear me, Farley?" Ronny asked. "I said it's because he is us." "Oh," I said softly. "I misheard you. I thought it was because we are 'is.'" "We are?" Ronny exclaimed in wonder and horror. I stared at the rocks behind him, my eyes blinking slowly before opening again. "Ronny," I whispered, "If we are 'is' and he is us, does that make him 'is' or does that make us him?" "Farley," Ronny suddenly gasped, "I think we're going to die." "No," I replied, shaking my head. "We haven't figured it out yet."

I could hear numerous noises in the background, but I couldn't discern if it was Delaney, Ellery, or something else trying to communicate with me. In an attempt to sharpen my hearing, I closed my eyes, but it only made everything disappear. I panicked when I realized that I couldn't hear without my sense of sight. I opened my eyes to find Ronny sitting upright, fidgeting with his hair. His disproportionately large eyes took up most of his face, bulging out to his forehead and down past his nose. I was horrified and in shock, but Ronny whispered softly, "What if there's nothing to figure out?" I turned around, my hands shaking uncontrollably and saw Delaney and Ellery. Ellery had put his hat back on, even though it didn't fit, and Delaney was staring at him with a combination of admiration and disgust. Ellery expressed his belief about the need to show no fear. However, I was fixated on Delaney, and was reminded of the first day we had made it to the clearing, where she seemed smaller, almost unreal, and was laughing on the ground. She had said to me, "You're all messed up, Farley...because of the hill..." I said, "We never got to move the boulder," to both the old and new Delaney. She looked through me, and as I stared at her, I noticed her hair wavering in the wind. It was then that I realized that she was more than what met the eye.

"Delaney," I asked desperately, "why aren't there any roses on the rosebushes?" She continued to stare blankly at me, and her eyes even turned briefly blood red. Confused, I attempted to repeat my question but my speech was impaired by the beer I had drank earlier. I persisted in my inquiry, only to have Delaney respond with a singsong question of her own: "Why should there be?" I then noticed that the boulders surrounding us had inexplicably grown larger, and I attempted to play music on them. Suddenly, the rocks began to shake, and the ground beneath us shook violently. I found myself floating above the clearing, watching as my friends reacted to the chaos. Delaney's expression was both cruel and kind, leaving me with a taste of bitterness and blood.

"Let me down," I gasped desperately. I closed my eyes and reopened them, realizing that I was back where I started and the rocks had stopped growing. Fear gripped me as I looked at Delaney. I tried to warn her, but found myself unable to speak. A sudden urge to be anywhere else overtook me, and I realized how horrible the situation was. And so, I ran. It felt as though the woods were chasing me, with emotions and sensations swirling around my head. Eventually, I collapsed behind a tree, hoping that no one would find me and trying to suppress the belief that salvation, deliverance, and destruction were all synonymous with the infiltration of my castle.

I wasn't sure exactly how time was passing or who was controlling it, or if it even existed for me at all. It didn't seem impossible that the universe had suspended time during the witch hunt, where I might somehow end up in the forest. As I stood there, I felt as though I was becoming a part of the forest, or it was becoming a part of me. A deep panic overcame me as I realized that I wasn't going to be saved by a search party, but absorbed by the universe. This slow and steady loss of myself and everything that defined me was terrifying. I felt as though I was screaming into silence - my voice disappeared into a void, a black hole of nothingness that engulfed everything. I then realized that I was lying on the ground, watching myself. I was part of everything, yet nothing at the same time. I was God and also the absence of God. I struggled to capture this moment, knowing it was futile, but still paralyzed by fear and amazement. Slowly, I floated back down to reality, but remained motionless for a long time, unable to shake the feeling of surrealness.

Slowly, I sat up, dazed and unsure if I had been absorbed by the Universe or if I had absorbed it. I was overcome by an inexplicable combination of serene tranquility and horrifying giddiness. The woods were pitch black except for the pale luminosity of the cool, placid moonlight that gently coated oddly shaped gaps on the ground. They sparkled strangely, and I approached one of the patches and stood there, gazing at the moon. Suddenly, I realized that the moon was not staring back at me. If I was somehow swallowed up by the universe, looking into the moon would be like looking at my own reflection. But could the moon see its reflection in me? Or was I somehow seeing mine in the moon? I turned and slowly walked through the woods. Whenever I stepped into a spot of moonlight, my skin flickered strangely, then slowly faded away, only to reappear when I returned to the shadows. The fear was replaced by fascination. I was no longer able to fear, and the sense of self that I had been cultivating disappeared. Hours passed as I walked towards Ronny Orwell to tell him what I had figured out. The woods seemed to circle around me, and I saw the same patches of moonlight. The taste of blood had transformed into a strange taste of silver fluorescence.

Finally, I was able to make out two familiar figures - they were the boulders. I headed towards them excitedly, watching them grow taller and taller, as they seemed to aid me in my attempt to reach them. I felt a deep connection with the forest, as if the entire woodland was racing towards the same destination, with the same fevered impulsivity and jubilance as I felt when confronting Ronny with the truth about what had happened. Despite the fact that the truth was even more horrific than we had originally imagined, things were absolutely, superbly euphoric. When I arrived at the clearing, it was almost completely dark, with the two boulders casting a shadow all around. Ronny was lying at the edge of the clearing, beside a tree, with his arms flung out to the sides. His hair was sticking to his forehead and neck, as sweat had covered his body and soaked through his clothing. I wasn't sure if he was truly there, as the moonlight continued to distort my vision. Trembling, I reached out and placed my hand on his shoulder. When he didn't respond, I gave him a good shaking. He recoiled and appeared frightened, his large eyes darting around the clearing. He grabbed my arm and stared at me for several moments. "Farley?" he whispered eventually. I just stared at him, watching the moonlight flicker and sparkle on his pale skin. "Listen, Ronny," I whispered, "You'll never believe what I've figured out." But with each passing moment, Ronny grew more and more alarmed, his eyes darting back and forth rapidly.

"Ronny," I hissed, feeling deep irritation at his poor attention span. "Where are they?" he despondently asked, wailing, "Where are they, Farley?". "Who?" I snapped, realizing the clearing was empty. "Delaney and Ellery must have gone somewhere else. Listen, that isn't important anymore," I said. "Not them," Ronny hissed, "Where are the Tralfamadorians?". "What?" I impatiently asked, noticing the moonlight playing strange tricks on his skin. "They were going to take me away and bring me to Tralfamadorians, Farley," he whispered. "You don't need to worry about that anymore," I encouraged, "Because, Ronny, you know what I've realized? We're God." "You mean the both of us?" Ronny asked slowly. "No," I snapped, "I am God of the Universe. But nobody else owns the Universe, Ronny, because it has chosen me as its God, just like yours will if you let it." Ronny stared at me before putting his face in his hands and sobbing, "The Tralfamadorians are gone, and you sound like a goddamn lunatic!". I felt irritated and tried to explain, but I noticed a headache and nausea. In the corner of my eye, I saw a pair of bottles lying in the clearing.

"Are those the same as the rest of the stuff we've been drinking tonight?" I trailed off, then swallowed. "Listen, Ronny. Are those the same as the rest of the drink we've had tonight?" He gave me an angry look. "You can't have them," he said. "Your fake friends took most of it, but I'm saving these two to give to Tralfamadorians as a sacrifice." His skin flickered green, then back to white. "Oh," I said, shaking my head. "But you do realize that the Tralfamadorians don't exist, right, Ronny?" "They do," he snapped. "They do exist, Farley, and you know it! You can't have it! Alright?" I was getting irritated that such a powerful substance was being saved for mythical creatures. "Listen, Ronny, it's beginning to wear off, and I need the feeling to last longer so I can finish figuring out—" Suddenly, Ronny tried to grab the bottles while I wasn't paying attention. Fortunately for me, he wasn't agile and I knocked the bottles out of his hands, pinning him to the ground. One rolled under the tree, and the other smashed into pieces on a rock. We were frozen for two seconds. Then, something inside me disconnected, and I felt uncontrollable hatred for Ronny Orwell in that moment. "Do you see what you've done?!" I shouted. The moon, forest, stars, and Earth poured their strength into me as I fought for ownership of the universe, for happiness, liberty, morality, power, truth, knowledge, deceit, escape, and understanding.

I could taste the sound of the blood pounding in my ears; of such strength was the sensation that I could feel it flowing downwards through my veins, into my arms, hands, fists, legs. I was never aware of having made the decision to attack Ronny; but the feeling of anger and hatred was such that there was a sense of insurmountable euphoria and triumph that came with its eventual release. Although I could not recall the point when it had begun, I was *incredibly* aware of the manner in which the rise and fall of my fists was causing the source of my anger such an incredible amount of pain, and causing *me* such an incredible amount of joy.

I was eventually aware of a point in time which he stopped struggling to get free; but I couldn't stop. It seemed to me that there was such an outpouring of blood from my heart to my fists that, were I to prevent it from being released, it would congeal up somewhere inside of me until eventually my chest would explode, leaving a mangled carcass spewing blood in its wake.

However, there came a point at which I caught a glimpse of Ronny's face; instead of sweat, his forehead was covered in blood; instead of pale, like the moonlight, it was turning ugly shades of red and dark purple. It was at this point that I realized I needed to stop. However, it was *also* at this point that I realized I couldn't.

Once I came to this realization, there were no traces of anger remaining; there was simply unstoppable, horrible *fear,* an emotion which I had very recently been sure certain I would never experience again.

It was as if the universe had taken my body captive; like before, in the woods, I was watching myself from an outside position. There was a deep, strange look of almost perfunctory concentration, enduring silently and eerily with each blow; and then, as I was jerked back into my body, I looked down at Ronny's and realized that it was no longer *his* face that I was attacking.

It was *mine.*

The chill that ran through my body should have stopped me right then and there, but I was no longer in control. Desperately, my mind called out to the earth and the universe, to everything over which I had proclaimed myself God, begging them to stop me. Tears ran down my face and onto the shirt of my victim as I sobbed in horror and desperation. I called out for help, shouting apologies, bargains, and prayers, but the universe refused to relinquish control of my body. It was then that I realized my body was not mine to control in the first place. As this realization hit me, my limbs began to go numb and my accuracy during the attack diminished. The blows became weaker and weaker until it felt like a lifetime of torture. Finally, I fell to the ground, panting and pleading silently with the moon, the sun, and the stars. I promised them I had learned my lesson and vowed to never let anyone in my castle again. After several moments, I forced myself to sit up. Ronny's face had returned to normal, but he was completely unconscious. I tapped his arm and called his name, but there was no response. I shook his shoulder and even climbed on top of him, shouting in his ear, but still, he did not wake up.

The momentary relief that I had previously experienced had completely evaporated. "Ronny, Ronny, hey kid, wake up. Are you there, you moron? There's no need to be like that," I screamed, trying to rouse him from unconsciousness. The moonlight created a strange spotlight on his face, highlighting the extent of the damage I had caused. My stomach dropped, and I was hit with a wave of nausea. I bent over and vomited for the second time in less than twelve hours, far away from Ronny. I returned to Ronny, shaking him and screaming in his ears, trying everything I could to wake him up. As he lay there, all I could think about was my future as a convict on the run. Suddenly, a beam of moonlight reflected off the broken beer glass and illuminated a tree nearby. I crawled under the tree, triumphant when I found the last unbroken bottle of beer. I got to my feet and uncapped the bottle, splashing it directly into Ronny's face. There was a moment of silence, which turned into panic when I heard his loud moan. But then, I felt a sense of immense relief when Ronny woke up and looked at me. However, the relief quickly dissolved when I saw the expression on his face, which was like that of an abused puppy. I wanted to apologize or thank him, but I wasn't good with words. All I could say was that my head hurt. Ronny nodded and wiped his face, revealing blood from his nose. Guilt washed over me. "Hey man, shouldn't we take you to the hospital or something?" I asked.

He stared at me before looking back at his hand and then returning his gaze to me once again. Then, he stood up, turned around, and began to walk away. "Ronny?" I said softly. "Where are you going?" He turned back to face me and replied with a sad and exhausted voice, "I'm going home. The Tralfamadorians obviously aren't coming." He turned away and resumed walking. As my eyes grew heavy, his figure became blurry.

"Ronny, that's dangerous. It's going to try and eat you like it did to me," I said, but the pain in my head became too intense to continue. I let out a sigh and rested my head on the ground. "I'm sorry that I was trying to break the windows," I whispered to the Earth, hoping it could hear me. I heard a rustling in the leaves, which I took as a form of grudging acceptance. I started apologizing for other things, and though I considered starting over, I eventually gave up and fell asleep under a boulder.

Chapter 16

When I woke up, I felt really awful. At first, I couldn't remember anything that had happened. Then, I convinced myself that Delaney was a serial killer who was going to attack me if I moved. I lay there for a while, feeling like someone had hit me on the head with an anvil. Eventually, I remembered what had happened and sat up, only to find that everyone else was gone. I grabbed the one intact beer bottle and started walking towards where Delaney had parked her car. But then I remembered the strange memory of stopping myself from attacking Ronny, and realized that he was missing. I called his name, but he didn't answer, and I started to panic. I ran towards the road, but was overcome by nausea and threw up. After recovering, I stumbled towards the road, regretting not following the trail back to Delaney's house because I didn't want to alert her mother to what had happened at our meeting.

I felt relieved when I saw Delaney's car parked on the side of the road. I ran towards it frantically but slowed my pace to a brisk walk when I remembered what had happened the last time. As I reached the car, I saw that Delaney and Ellery had spent the entire night in the back seat and had fallen asleep on top of each other. Angry, I knocked on the window to wake them up. Delaney woke up first and moved to the front seat. When I asked her if she had seen Ronny, she snapped at me for my breath still smelling like vomit. I told her I threw up again and asked if she and Ellery had seen Ronny walk by. She shook her head while giving me a look of disbelief and told me what he had done to their drinks. When Ellery woke up, he asked if Delaney was killing people. I interrupted and asked if he had seen Ronny.

Ellery yawned and asked, "Last night?" But Delaney snapped suddenly and told them to get out of her car. They both turned to stare at her, confused. Delaney threatened them with mace and demanded they leave before she counted to ten. Not wanting to anger her more, they left and walked away. Delaney threw a balled-up piece of paper at Ellery as she drove away. The note said she was leaving the club, which angered Ellery. The protagonist tried to console him and told him it was never a club, but a society. Ellery then called his brother to come pick them up.

"So," Paul said, pulling up in the car, "you got hammered, I see?" He looked at the bottle I was holding in my hand. "Not exactly," Ellery muttered. Paul watched as the two of us got into the car. "What exactly happened then?" Neither of us said anything. Ellery appeared incredibly interested in the polyester on the back of the seat. "Come on, Ellie," Paul said cheerily, "you aren't going to tell me anything?" I glared up at Paul. "You know, we're people, not artwork," I said. Paul raised his eyebrows and turned to start the car. "Nice friends you've got there, Ellie," he said, not for the first time. "He isn't really my friend, Paul," Ellery said. "But in all honesty, he does have a point." Since I wasn't in the mood to go home, I asked Paul to drop me off at Ronny's house instead. The front door was slightly open, which I took as a positive sign that Ronny had made it home. However, I couldn't remember if we had closed the door on our way out; the experience was becoming blurry and confused. I pushed open the door and entered the house. "Ronny?" I called out with a slight sense of trepidation. "Hello? Are you alive?" I began to wonder what I would do if he hadn't made it home. I began to get worried and thought that I should have tried harder to find him in the forest because the chances of him walking home in his condition were probably pretty slim. I began to conspire various ways in which I could excuse myself just in case he had suffered any severe injury, but then I heard a noise from upstairs. I jogged up the staircase quickly, calling out his name. I heard noises coming from the other end of the hall, so I started walking in that direction. Once I had ascertained that he was alive, I decided I was going to go home so I could puke on my mother's shoes and put an end to the whole experience.

When I arrived at the door where the noise was coming from, I knocked politely, even though it was already partly open. "Ronny?" I called again. I could hear his voice inside, but it didn't sound like he was talking to me. He appeared to be muttering to someone frantically, as if he didn't want anyone from the outside to hear. I hesitated for a moment and considered leaving; after all, he had made it home, hadn't he? But something forced me to push the door open - some strange, inquisitive part of my personality that I had yet to come into contact with until that very moment. I stepped into the room and stared. He was sitting alone in a bathtub that was completely devoid of water, wearing nothing but a pair of green and white plaid boxers. Empty beer bottles and cans littered the floor, but he couldn't have been that drunk because it seemed to me like he had spilled the majority of it onto the bathmat, which was soaking wet, and onto himself. He turned to look at me with eyes like a rabbit cornered in a hole by a fox. I blinked and stared at him again, looking around in complete shock. "Ronny," I said, my tone somewhere between disgust and admiration, "how are you still drinking that stuff?" He started giggling madly, slowly raising a trembling finger and pointing it in my direction. "You," he snickered, his voice coming out thinner and higher than usual, "look awful." I glanced down at my shirt. There was a significant amount of dirt on it, as well as stains of beer and strange smudges of red which were most likely Ronny's blood. My hands were scratched and my jeans had a large rip in them, exposing a bloody knee. But then I shook my head, looked back at him and said: "speak for yourself." He blinked several times, then held up his hands very close to his face. "You- you've got to get out of here, Farley," he mumbled. He took a sip of his drink, then immediately started coughing and spit it back out again.

"I asked Ronny, 'What exactly was in those drinks?' He started shaking his head slowly and muttering, 'I don't know, Sam told me not to drink them, but I wanted you to like me and help you with your castle.' I reassured him that he had helped me a little, not wanting to make him feel any worse. Ronny then asked if the imaginary creatures he saw were coming. I sadly told him that they weren't real. He became angry and shouted that it didn't matter if they were real because they made him happy. He then seemed to be arguing with himself, muttering about leaving and joining the creatures."

"I have to..." I said, my voice rising several octaves higher than usual, to Ronny. "No, listen," he muttered, still talking to himself. "Either way, it's a win. If it's different, it'll be better. If it's nothing, it won't matter. If it's different or if it's nothing, it'll be better... it won't matter..." My body froze up and I suddenly had an overwhelming desire to leave the room and never look back. I wanted to get as far away from Ronny and his house as possible, wash my hands of all responsibility and free my mind of any hold that Ronny had ever had on me. But I couldn't move any of my limbs and my breaths were coming in and out strangely, as if my lungs were struggling to breathe. Finally, Ronny looked at me with pure hatred and despair. It was a gaze of ultimate abhorrence and also a desperate plea for help. His eyes seemed to jumpstart my body into motion and I began walking backwards as fast as I could. "Bye, Ronny," I gasped, taking the final step backwards and slamming the door shut. I stood there for a moment, feeling the strength of his gaze holding me in place, then slowly turned my back and inhale deeply to see if my lungs were still working. Finally, I ran. I didn't pay attention to my direction, all I knew was that I wanted to get as far away from that house as possible and never, never look back.

I made it out to the road again and started walking blindly—I could feel the fear and the horror and the nausea all culminating together in my stomach—I had to pause on the side of the road to throw up again, except that *this* time my stomach was so empty that the result was nothing but a bunch painful, awful, gagging. Mindlessly, I stumbled forwards; I didn't want to call anyone to come get me; I didn't want to *see* anyone again, ever—it was too sickening, too painful, too *horrible*—and so it wasn't till I had *gotten* there that I realized where I had been going.

The hill loomed up at me like an old friend and a terrible enemy; the awful realization that I had just walked in almost a complete *circle* made me feel the true extent of my idiocy like a metal bucket smashed against my head. Slowly, as if in a daze, I started to ascend; trying to justify my logic, I told myself that it made absolutely *perfect* sense, because I was going to ask Delaney to drive me back home; but really, I knew that wasn't what it was.

I needed something from her that I had been seeking since the first time I'd walked up the hill; I needed an *answer*.

The walk wasn't as difficult as I'd thought it would be; my body seemed to have reached a point where it was in such an incredible amount of pain that anything further was just a dull, numbing pang; the only difficulty arose when I was almost to the very top, and I stumbled and tripped. This fall brought me to the strangest realization; that I was still carrying the empty beer bottle from the clearing, having forgotten about its existence until it fell out of my hands and rolled off to the side of the road. I picked it up and continued to walk.

I had begun to dread knocking on the door to Delaney's house and therefore possibly encountering her mother; however, once her house came into full view, I realized that this wouldn't be an issue. I saw Delaney's form bent over the garden at the front of her house, her arms moving back and forth very rapidly, her hair falling all around her face in a wild and frightening jumble.

In a daze, I walked closer and closer to her until I was standing right next to her; and that was when I noticed what she was doing; although *really* it was something I had known all along.

Sweat glistened from her brow as she continued her frantic tearing; blood ran down her fingers and dripped slowly down her wrists and arms, me standing several feet behind her in a strange trance of reverence and fear. The empty rosebush; which I had originally assumed strangely incapable of growing flowers; had begun to sprout tiny buds, hidden cloistered among large and foreboding thorns which curved outwards to protect them. Delaney didn't seem to care; she continued tirelessly, reaching her arms deeper and deeper into the rosebush to pull out the buds that had been growing there, which the frantic desperation of someone clawing their way out of an inescapable abyss.

Even as I took a step closer, she didn't seem to notice me. Such was the intensity of her focus on the roses, that I shook my head slowly back and forth. I was gripped by the sight of something terrible but couldn't understand why. Eventually, I said "Delaney" in a voice filled with wonder and confusion. She whipped around and examined me with a furious, wild gaze. I felt irrational fear that she would attack me. "What are you doing here?" she snapped angrily, with malignity in her eyes. "I told you that I quit." I took a step closer and said, "I know. But you never did tell me what it is that you hate so much about these roses." She stared at me for a moment, and I felt a stroke of fear as I realized I might have asked something I shouldn't have. Eventually, she pushed her hair out of her face, leaving a red streak of blood on her forehead, and said, "Ask Ellery." Then she continued her mission, and I watched in horror. As I turned to leave, my foot got caught in a pothole, and I fell flat on my face. Clutching an empty beer bottle to my chest, I lay there panting. Suddenly, I heard someone say my name. It was Delaney's mother, who had been staring at me from the doorway. She crouched beside me, offering me her hand.

"Mrs. Fowles," I said shakily, sounding embarrassingly close to tears, "What's wrong with Delaney?" I saw my reflection in her face and noticed a confused and helpless expression which matched my own. She took my hand and pulled me up to my feet. "Ma'am," I muttered, "I'm sorry. My name is Farley." Then I burst into tears. She guided me towards the house, away from the road. She did not look at Delaney as she led me to the porch and sat me down. Delaney continued to desperately tear at the rosebushes, appearing frantic and hopeless. "Everything's going to be alright, Farley," Mrs. Fowles said soothingly, although she did not understand the extent of the situation. "It's time for you to go home." I do not remember much of the ride home, except for feeling nauseous and silent. All I could think was that I did not want to throw up in Mrs. Fowles' car. When we arrived back at my house, Mrs. Fowles asked kindly if I wanted her to come in with me. "No," I whispered. "Thank you, very much." I stumbled out of the car. "I just need to..." I shook my head slowly. "I need to go in myself." Despite my wishes, Mrs. Fowles got out of her car and helped me walk to the door. She knocked several times until my mother answered. She was preoccupied with her book club and took a few moments to answer the door. "Hello!" my mother called cheerily. "It's lovely to meet you. You must be..." Her smile faded as she made eye contact with me. "Farley, dear," she said. "Why aren't you in school?" Her eyes traveled to the beer bottle still in my hand. "Farley, what's going on?" she whispered.

"I'm Mary Fowles," Mrs. Fowles told my mother, "And I think your son might be sick." "You think he's..." my mother trailed off, frowning at me. "Is he...is he..." She made eye contact with Mrs. Fowles and nodded towards the empty bottle in my hand. "Well, Mrs. Underwood," Delaney's mother said, "I think you need to ask your son yourself." She nodded at my mother, gave me an odd sort of pat on the shoulder, and then turned around and walked away. "So...so you're sick, Farley?" my mother said loudly, raising her eyebrows. "Well, dear, why don't you just go lie down upstairs? I'll bring you something to drink. You just...Farley!" I pushed past her and walked into the kitchen where the book club was sitting, clenching the empty bottle tightly in my hand. Their eyes widened when they saw me and they stared at me, speechless. "Don't you people ever leave?" I demanded in a strange, hollowed-out voice. My mother hurried up to me and grabbed my hand. "Farley is very sick," she explained. "He doesn't mean that at all. Farley, dear, come upstairs and I—" "LISTEN!" I felt the exclamation erupt from somewhere deep inside my throat, casting all four of the women into stunned and absolute silence. And then, with a motion that seemed somehow irrepressible and unavoidable, I brought my arm back and flung the empty beer bottle at the opposite kitchen wall. Instead of hitting the cabinet, as I had intended, it veered to the right and smashed through the window, the sound of tinkling glass permeating the ears of the horrified onlookers long after any audible noise had ceased.

I turned to my mother, who was staring at me with a strange expression of terrified anger. However, I noticed with a sense of hopeless despair that there was just the right amount of indignation, shock, and concern behind it. But, behind those emotions, there was a hardened core of muted nothingness and sterile apathy. "I've broken all the windows," I said. "There's nothing else I can do." Then, I turned away from the four of them and walked up the stairs without looking back. There was nothing to see anyways.

Chapter 17

When I arrived at school the next day, I couldn't find Delaney or Ronny anywhere. Upon my arrival, I surveyed the parking lot and noticed that Delaney's car was nowhere to be seen. I searched for Ronny in the library, but was reminded that I was still banned from the library after being chased out by a furious librarian. As I walked down the hallway, Ellery approached me dressed in all black without his glasses. He asked if we were still friends and I responded with a remark about how we are no longer a society. He then asked if I had spoken to Delaney and I avoided the question by asking if he knew why she hated her rosebushes. When he asked me to tell her he was sorry, I responded that she probably wouldn't talk to me either. Ellery then gave me his hat and told me to keep it, despite us never really being friends.

I looked at the hat and spoke to Ellery, "How many times do I have to tell you that your hat is ugly, and I don't want it?" Ellery's face showed a mix of anger and amusement. "Well," he said, "you're taking it anyways." He forcefully put the hat on my head, covering my entire face. I wanted to respond angrily, but I knew my words would be muffled, defeating the purpose. I heard Ellery's footsteps as he walked away. The bell rang, but I didn't feel like going to class. Instead, I headed towards the janitor's closet, hoping to find Ronny but knowing he wouldn't be there. When I arrived, I knocked loudly on the door. Steve the janitor opened it and looked at me. "Have you seen Ronny today?" I asked him. He shook his head, and I felt disappointed. I offered him Ellery's hat, and he raised his eyebrows in confusion. "Thank you, kid," he said, "but I don't want that." I insisted he take it anyway, and he reluctantly accepted it. He stared at me and said, "You're that kid... the one who asked me to look through the garbage cans." I nodded and said, "I know it doesn't make sense, but if you did, we would be happy." He looked at me suspiciously and said, "Why don't you look through the trash cans then?" I decided not to try and explain anymore and said goodbye, but Steve called out to me in anger, asking me why I didn't answer his question. I grinned and said, "Don't be an idiot, it doesn't work like that."

-The End-